Text Me on Tuesday

An Accidentally in Love Story
Book 1

Whitney Dineen & Melanie Summers

Also by Whitney Dineen

Romantic Comedies
Love is a Battlefield
Ain't She Sweet
It's My Party
You're so Vain (coming soon)
The Event
The Move
The Plan
The Dream
Relatively Normal
Relatively Sane
Relatively Happy
The Reinvention of Mimi Finnegan
Mimi Plus Two
Kindred Spirits
She Sins at Midnight
Going Up?
Love for Sale (coming soon)

Non-Fiction Humor
Motherhood, Martyrdom & Costco Runs

Conspiracy Thriller
See No More

Middle Reader Fiction
Wilhelmina and the Willamette Wig Factory
Who the Heck is Harvey Stingle?

Children's Books
The Friendship Bench

Also by Melanie Summers

ROMANTIC COMEDIES
The Crown Jewels Series
The Royal Treatment
The Royal Wedding
The Royal Delivery

Paradise Bay Series
The Honeymooner
Whisked Away
The Suite Life
Resting Beach Face

Crazy Royal Love Series
Royally Crushed
Royally Wild
Royally Tied (Coming Soon)

WOMEN'S FICTION
The After Wife
The Deep End

STEAMY OFFERINGS by MJ Summers
The Full Hearts Series
Break in Two
Breaking Love
Breaking Clear
Breaking Hearts
The Break-up

Text Me on Tuesday

An Accidentally in Love Story
Book 1

Whitney Dineen & Melanie Summers

DEDICATION

Dedicated to my Big Hollywood Daddy Scott Schwimer.
Friend. Mentor. Well-dressed protector of dreams.
Xoxo,
Whitney

And to Dolly Parton,
Who reminds us all to appreciate what we've got,
make the most of what we're given,
help any way we can,
and be kind.
Thank you,
Melanie

A Behind the Scenes Look at the Birth of a New Series…

(Don't worry. It's not gory.)

Hey Mel, I want to write a mistaken identity texting romcom, but I don't have time, so you have to write it with me. 🙏

I also have no time, but tell me more because it sounds really fun (and I'm in serious need of fun on account of my broken wrist, full-house reno, and being trapped in my house with my three kids for the past year).

Boohoo, we have our sad story. NYC caterer meets an uptight, snooty business man… naked. 🍑

Oooh! I'm intrigued. Can he be British?

If that sells it for you… 🎩🕴️✓

It does!

God save the queen! 🇬🇧

When do you want to start? 🥂

We've already started… sending first chapter now. 😊

😊 That is SO you! This is gonna be fun!

Chapter One

Aimée

"Hey, Aimes, you want to grab a mani-pedi after our shift?" my friend Teisha asks while hurrying past me to the pastry display.

"You bet," I answer while changing the filter on the coffee maker and starting a new pot. "'Cause you know I have an extra fifty bucks burning a hole in my pocket."

"Not this again." She flings a bear claw on a plate. "I know you're trying to get your catering business going. Got it. But you have to live, girl! Do something nice for yourself occasionally."

"I did something nice for myself yesterday, T. I paid my electric bill," I say, bagging a cranberry orange muffin for a to-go order. The truth is my feet are begging me to say yes to the pedicure after close to eight hours straight rushing around on them.

"I'm going to say it again. My brother is moving out of my place next week and I'd rather have you for a roommate than anyone else in this world." She bats her eyelashes at me, causing the whites of her eyes to shine brightly against the frame of her flawless ebony skin.

"I just don't want our living together to affect our friendship," I say, even though I've been giving serious consideration to her offer lately. I'm running out of money and I'm not getting enough catering jobs to get my new business up and running fast enough to save the sinking ship that is my life.

"I don't know how you can stand living in that shoe box you call an apartment. I'd be ready for the funny farm after one night. It's like a prison cell." She convulses in a full body shiver for effect.

Teisha has accurately described my home. When I moved to New York City from Rochester last year, I was sure my catering business would thrive here, just like it had upstate. I was sure I'd be moving on up to the East Side, a la *The Jeffersons* theme song from that old TV show my parents liked to watch.

That has not been the case.

Even though I came to the Big Apple with enough money to pay my rent for a year, I had to take a waitressing job at the bakery to cover my other expenses—electric, phone, toilet paper, the occasional new tube of lipstick. I've only bought two since I've been here.

I ran out of rent money last month and had to start digging into my savings. Which will not last, with the price of Manhattan real estate such as it is. "When is Terrance leaving?" I ask.

"Five days, but you can move in any time and share my room until he's gone. That way you won't have to pay an extra month's rent."

I exhale like I'm trying to blow out birthday candles at the far end of Yankee stadium. "I'll do it. I'm month to month now, so I can leave at any time." As I refill the coffee creamers, I add, "But only if you're sure."

My friend throws her Amazonian arms around me and jumps up and down, causing the top of my head to bump against her chin. "All right! We're gonna have the best damn time there ever was!"

"You're a good friend," I tell her as I push her away to wipe off the cream that's now running down my apron.

"Hurry up and finish what you're doing. Then we can clock out and celebrate by getting our nails done. After that, we'll hit the Red Apple for a bottle of wine."

I'm feeling all kinds of things at the moment—relief, trepidation, excitement. It's like I'm standing in the middle of a hurricane of emotion looking for something solid to hold on to. When I can't find it, I decide to grab ahold of optimism as it flies by and see where it carries me.

On the D train up to Harlem, Teisha asks, "How did your date go last night? You never told me."

Rolling my eyes, I reach out for one of the many stripper poles running down the aisle of the subway car—I've recently started calling them that after a flash mob of pole dancers came into the car I was riding last month. If you catch the video on YouTube, I'm the curvy blonde in the corner doing a facial impersonation of a mounted fish. You know, wide open eyes and a mouth the perfect "O" of shock and awe.

"My date was typical," I tell my friend. "Wanna-be-young businessman who thinks he's about to take over the world, takes me to an expensive restaurant and suggests I only order off the appetizer side. Then, after spending the whole meal talking about himself, he pays the check, leaving a ten percent tip—I looked. Then we get into a cab and he gives the driver *his* address."

"Oooooooh, slimy. What happened when you told him you weren't going home with him?" she asks, rubbing her hands together so quickly you'd think she was trying to start a fire *Survivor*-style.

"He had the cabbie pull over and then told me if he wasn't going to get an immediate return on his investment, I could find another way home."

"Why that no-good dirty dog! What did you do?"

"I got out. But not before telling him he needed a stronger mouthwash and that only letting his date order appetizers for dinner was like having a tattoo that says 'Cheapy McTightwad' on his forehead."

The construction worker standing next to me wants to know, "What would have happened if he took you out for chicken and waffles?"

I shoot him a conspiratorial look and lie, "I would have been able to tell my friend here what his apartment looked like."

Our pole mate laughs uproariously. "Honey, if I wasn't already married, I'd be offering to take you out for that chicken right now."

Ignoring the intruder in our conversation, Teisha warns, "He better not have the nerve to set foot in Bean Town again or I'm going to spice up his coffee with some hot sauce."

"Guys like him never return to the scene of the crime when they've been dissed. Their fragile male egos can't handle it."

Getting out at 110th St., we walk three blocks to Teisha's favorite nail salon called The Finger. We amble into the shop under the giant, neon-flashing sign of a hand flipping the bird.

"Kwan," Teisha calls out, "we need the works. All four paws with gel and nail art. We're celebrating here!"

Teisha has a little crush on Kwan, who emigrated here from Korea ten years ago. He gives off a sensitive, if not mysterious vibe. As talented as he is with nails, the man could seriously get women to pay him to just stare at him all day. Did I mention he was good looking? In heavily accented English, the handsome man in the salon tells her, "My name is Kevin, not Kwan."

"Uh-huh," Teisha replies, "and I'm Queen Latifah. Use your real name, man. Be proud of your roots!"

Kevin/Kwan turns to the woman next to him and tells her something in Korean. She motions me to a massage chair. While the hot water pours in, soothing my aching feet, my phone pings, alerting me of a new email message.

If I weren't desperately hoping it was a prospective new client, I would have ignored it and let Calgon take me away.

Instead, I pull out my phone and read:

Miss Tompkins,

I've received your many flyers in the mail and am intrigued not only by your persistence, but also by your menu. Our caterer unexpectedly dropped out of a corporate lunch we need served at our headquarters on Wall Street tomorrow. If you can help us out with this and my boss is happy with the food, I would be happy to steer more work your way.

Byron Scott

Executive Assistant to Noel Fitzwilliam

Fitzwilliam & Assoc.

I let out of whoop of joy so loud, Teisha says, "Girl, I almost tinkled in my drawers, and I'm not sure Kwan here would appreciate having to clean up that kind of mess. What in the world are you yelling about?"

"Mani/pedis are on me!" I shout. "I just got my first in with Fitzwilliam & Associates! You're gonna have to count me out for that bottle of wine tonight, Teish. When I'm done here, I'm going straight to the grocery store and start prepping for tomorrow's luncheon."

I get busy sending a reply message to Byron, accepting the job and asking for details. Then I mentally start to prepare a list of all the tasks I need to complete to be ready in time. My grandma Jane used to warn about counting my chickens before they hatched, but I'm not worried. I have a feeling my fortune is about to change.

Chapter Two

Noel

"All right, team, I think that's it for changes. I want to thank you all for busting your arses—as we say in England—for the last eight plus months." I offer what I'm told is a rare smile to the twelve haggard staff members seated around the enormous polished mahogany conference room table. "Before I let you go, I do have a few things to say. I know I don't have to tell you that tomorrow is the most important pitch of most of our careers, certainly mine anyway. One Rosenthal is the reason I made the trek across the pond and set up shop here last year. This tower will be the crown jewel of the Manhattan skyline—a shining beacon of the future of architecture here in the center of the universe. The tower will be luxurious yet with environmentally-conscious finishings and design, as well as cutting-edge technology.

"It's going to earn Fitzwilliam & Associates our rightful place on the world stage. Should we succeed tomorrow—and I believe we will—we'll become one of the most sought-after architectural firms on the globe. Decades worth of work will come from this one monumental project." I pause and steady my voice before I allow myself to sound excited. "We've done the work, now the final piece of the puzzle is to ensure we put our best foot forward tomorrow, or feet I suppose, since there are several of us."

There's a polite chuckle from around the room, but it's not because I'm funny. It's because I pay their rent. I'm relatively certain they all hate me, but I literally couldn't care less. I didn't get where I am today by worrying about winning popularity contests. "Tomorrow, skip the perfumes and colognes. Mr. Brown Senior is allergic to them and we don't need him to be *at all* distracted from our message. And please, when you get in here, no fidgeting, no sniffling, no worried expressions. We must present ourselves calmly and confidently as we usher in this new era of design."

I glance over at my highly distractible twin brother, Byron, who has served as my long-time executive assistant. Byron and I may be twins, but we are nothing alike. Other than having identical noses (which we got from our mother, thank God, because our father has quite the honker) and similar smiles, most people don't think we're brothers, let alone twins. He has sandy brown hair while mine is almost black. His eyes are dark blue, mine are light green. He's Mr. Goodtime and I'm Mr. Responsible, who employs Mr. Goodtime in order to keep him from ruining the family name by becoming a male stripper (which he announced as his true calling just after we blew out the candles on our eighteenth birthday cake).

That was eighteen years ago, and his ideas haven't gotten much better since.

Byron isn't exactly what you'd call detail-oriented (a bit of a negative in an assistant, to be honest) but he's one of two people on this planet that I trust explicitly (the other one being me). Byron uses his middle name Scott as his last name (as requested by our father, the great Lord Fitzwilliam shortly after Byron came out to the family), and yes, dear old dad is a complete wanker and neither of us will likely ever forgive him. Well, Byron might, but I certainly won't.

As with most awful things in life, there is a silver lining to Byron having a different last name—it has allowed him to serve as a spy of sorts on my behalf. People *love* him—he's friendly, laid-back, and easy to talk to (unlike me), so they often dish about how much they hate me, whether they're planning to quit, screw me over, and/or if they'd like to 'choke the crap out of me and dump my body in the Thames' (as one of my former junior architects put it). So, even though he screws up nearly as often as he gets things right, I gladly keep him around because there is no price that can be put on trust. I know, I've tried to buy it before.

At the moment, however, my brother is completely undermining my words by allowing himself to be openly engrossed in whatever is happening on his mobile phone. I tap the spot on the table in front of him and say, "And don't even think about bringing your mobile devices into tomorrow's presentation. We don't want to seem as though anything is more important than the client, including whatever's going on this week on *RuPaul's Drag Race*."

That worked. Byron snaps to attention. "I'm sorry, what were you saying?"

I point to his phone. "Leave that at your desk during the meeting tomorrow."

He shoots me a satisfied smile. "You are about to love both me and my little friend here," he says, shaking his phone at me. "I just received an invitation to the Dropbox holding the entire pitch Lassiter and Sons gave today."

I freeze and blink a few times while I let that sink in. Lassiter and Sons is our main competition on this bid, and, until this moment, they've had the upper hand (since WL Brown Senior is godfather to Lassiter Junior's eldest boy). It's like someone handing you the answer key the night before your calculus exam at university. "How exactly did you manage that?"

"One of the draftsmen over there has a bit of a crush on yours truly," he says with a shrug. "And to be honest, in this case, taking one for the team wouldn't exactly be a burden, if you catch my drift."

The few female employees at the table giggle. Women tend to want Byron to apply for the position of gay best friend—believing he'll be just the thing to boost their flailing self-esteem and help them unlock the code to finding the perfect man.

"Wow, I can't believe someone sent that to you," my most junior of the junior architects, Jack Layton, says, scooting his chair closer to Byron's. "Let's see what they've got."

"Yes, let's," Byron says with a satisfied grin. If there's one thing Byron loves, it's being the center of attention, and with this little bombshell, he has most certainly captured the imaginations of a dozen people who, only moments ago, looked too exhausted to breathe.

Cindy Pruitt, one of our project managers, speaks up from the far side of the table. "Wait. We're not going to look at it, are we? That's got to be some violation of some sort, right?"

Oh, Cindy, why do you have to go all Jiminy Cricket on me? Can't we just take this one advantage and go straight to the top? I'll just never look at myself in the mirror again. It'll be fine.

No, it won't. Damn. She's right.

It takes everything in me to shake my head and force myself to say, "No, of course not. That's not how we do business."

"Are you kidding me?" Jack asks, sitting back in his chair. "You said it yourself—this is *the* most important pitch of our lives. If we've got an edge, we'd be stupid not to use it."

Double damn. He's also not wrong. Having access to the materials they've chosen, the design itself, *and* their fees would easily allow us to make adjustments that would solidify our position as front-runner for this job. This is one of those moments when valuing your integrity sucks overcooked Brussels sprouts. Turning to my brother, I say, "Do not accept the invitation. Do not. Tell him you appreciate it, but no."

As an afterthought, I add, "You have my blessing to still 'take one for the team' if you so desire. Just don't tell me about it."

"Are you serious, Noel?" senior architect Ali Burman says. "I don't know if this is how they do business in London, but in New York, it's dog eat dog. I've got four teenagers, Noel. *Four.* They're going to break me financially between dance classes, baseball camps, saving for college ... not to mention the food bill. Do you know what it costs to feed four teenagers?"

"Twelve-hundred a month," a few of the people at the table say.

Ali's head snaps back, and Byron says, "You may have mentioned it."

"Sorry, Ali, but I don't think it's worth the risk," Cindy says. "I mean, what if we got caught?"

"We're not going to get caught," I say, as eleven sets of hopeful eyes turn to me. "Because we're not going to do it. Delete the email immediately. We're not trading our integrity for a job. Even if it is the biggest, most incredible project we'll ever bid on and it's the type of legacy every architect dreams of having." Rats, I'm talking myself out of doing the right thing. *No, Noel. Stop that.* "What we are going to do is win this thing *without* cheating or undercutting someone else's bid *or* stealing their ideas. We don't have to stoop so low because we've put together the best team in the city. Plus, we've checked off every box the client is asking for and then some."

I glance around at their faces, giving them my best impression of an ultra-confident CEO. The response is underwhelming to say the least. "Okay, I say we call it a night. Go home and do whatever it is you do that helps you relax and recharge. Hopefully by this time tomorrow night, we'll be celebrating. Thanks, everyone."

Murmurs of relief and the closing clicks of laptops bounce off the glass walls of the floor-to-ceiling windows. A quick glance at the East River and the Brooklyn skyline behind it tells me it's late evening. A single ferry crosses the dark shimmering waters of the river, taking the last of the haggard suits home for the night. I pick up my pen and jot some notes on a pad of graph paper while my weary staff slowly make their way out of the room. I don't dare look up because that would mean facing the utter disappointment in their eyes. I'm fighting every impulse I have to grab Byron's phone and download the presentation, and I don't need to see Ali's let-down expression as he slinks home to his brood of hungry children.

Cindy stops beside me on her way out. "You did the right thing," she says, touching my forearm in a way that makes me wish I had left the sleeves of my dress shirt rolled down today.

I give her a quick nod and a distant smile. "I appreciate your vote of confidence."

"I'm not sure if it was the *smart* thing. I mean, we probably won't win the bid now, but it'll help you avoid prison time anyway." She shakes her head at me. "I had a cousin who went to jail for tax evasion. I don't think you'd do well in that sort of environment."

Brilliant. "I don't think I'd go to—never mind. Have a lovely evening, Cindy."

Byron is the only one who remains, tapping away on his phone. "Do you need me to stick around, boss?" His use of the word "boss" is done in the same vein that hipsters grow beards—ironically. "What are the chances that you're going to actually leave here before midnight?"

"Slim to none."

"Great," he says with a sigh.

"I'm not asking you to stay."

"Yes, I know, but that dreamy jazz musician asked me to dinner and I won't enjoy it nearly as much if I know you're here toiling away into the wee hours all by yourself."

"Shall I pretend I'm going home too so you can feel better?"

"That would be lovely," he says, gathering up his laptop and water bottle.

I stand, collect my things, and follow him down the long hall to my corner office here on the forty-second floor of the Liberty Bank Tower—the building that says to the world, *I've made it*. Byron stops at his desk and drops off his laptop.

I'm just about to bid him a good night when I remember one last thing he was meant to take care of for me. "Byron, I just want to make sure you've got the catering all set up for tomorrow."

"Yes, of course," he says in his how-dare-you tone. "What do you take me for?"

"It's just that occasionally you get sidetracked," I say as gently as possible.

He picks up his messenger bag and gives me a steely glare. "Do you really think I don't know how to host a party?"

"I would never question your hosting abilities. But I overheard you earlier this afternoon when you slammed your hands on your desk and shouted, 'The bloody caterer pulled out!'"

Byron rolls his eyes. "What kind of assistant would I be if I didn't have a long list of catering companies at my disposal?"

"So, you found someone," I say, giving him a pointed look.

"Obviously," he huffs.

"And it's not just some rando who happened to drop off a flyer?"

Planting one hand on his hip, Byron says, "I am officially offended. I know how important this meeting is. As if I would entrust something of this magnitude to just anyone."

Here we go. "That's not what I said. I just need everything to be absolutely perfect tomorrow."

"I assure you I will have an elegantly laid out, absolutely delectable lunch for the clients. The company I chose is extremely professional and highly regarded throughout the city. Now, if there's nothing else, I would like to go home and shower before my date."

"Go," I say with a nod. "Have fun."

He hurries away, calling over his shoulder, "I won't tell you to do the same because we both know you have no clue what that word means."

"Fun doesn't pay the bills," I say as the elevator doors open and Byron steps on.

He spins around, hits the button, and announces, "Life is for making memories. Not money."

The doors close, giving him the last word, but for once, I don't care. I'm too tired to think of a good comeback. Sighing, I walk over to my desk and open my laptop, something about his words scratching at my insides. Dropping into my chair, I mutter, "I know what fun means. Maybe I just have a different definition of it than most people."

I open the presentation file to go over it one last time with a fine-toothed comb. "You know what'll be fun? Watching WL Brown Senior sign the contract tomorrow afternoon. That'll be a riot."

I hope.

Chapter Three

Aimée

I barely got any sleep last night. I'm fueled entirely by adrenaline and caffeine, but it's a combination that's never done me wrong. I stayed up until two in the morning cutting up fruit, and marinating vegetables for the roasted veggie and herbed goat cheese baguettes I'm serving.

I woke up at five to grill the peppers, eggplant, and onions, before assembling the sandwiches and rolling them tightly in plastic wrap so the flavors could continue to blend.

Byron, my contact at Fitzwilliam & Associates, told me they want upscale sandwiches to be served alongside two salads and some kind of fresh fruit. All desserts should be in the cookie family. His last email said:

And dear God, no crisps! No one wants to sit in a conference room surrounded by crunching.

Byron must be English to call chips crisps. I'm determined to give him the best catered lunch he's ever had, even if it means lessening my profit margin. If I can reel in a steady client, I can gradually increase my prices to market rate.

Teisha calls at seven sharp. "I covered my shift so I can help you today. When do you need me there?"

"You're a life saver, Teish! Can you come to my place and help me load everything into the van?" I brought my catering truck with me from Rochester with fantasies of racing all over Manhattan and Brooklyn filling my head. So far it's left its parking space under my building a grand total of four times. One of those times was to get gas.

"You want me to come now?" she asks.

"Yes, please. You're the best, T. I'll see you soon." I hang up and hurry to my closet, locking for the perfect thing to wear. In Rochester, I usually went with the stereotypical black dress pants and white shirt. It wasn't important that I looked like anything other than I was there.

But here in New York, I feel like I need to be super-chic and more refined. You know, like the kind of person who works for the satisfaction of a job well done and not because I'm running low on toilet paper. Which I am.

I settle on a navy wrap dress that hugs my generous curves without looking slutty. Then I roll my long blonde hair into a french twist, releasing a couple of wavy tendrils to avoid looking severe.

After putting on a pair of low heels, I check myself out in the mirror that's wedged behind the bathroom door. I want to say that I look like a movie star from the fifties—sexy, feminine, and alluring.

But the truth is, I'm giving off a modern-day Mary Poppins vibe. *Why is that?*

I decide it's my matronly footwear that no other twenty-eight-year-old on the planet would be caught dead in. I throw a pair of higher heels into my bag so that I can put them on before serving lunch.

I pull out two aprons with the company logo for Nibbles and Noshes on them—the three words all caterers have to remember are, "advertise, advertise, advertise!" Once that's done, I start checking things off my list of everything that has to go down to the van.

Teisha arrives wearing her work uniform, black pants and a white polo. She takes one look at me and says, "You look efficient."

"What's that supposed to mean?" Because it sure doesn't sound like a compliment.

"You look nice, professional," she decides with her head cocked to the side.

"Do I look like Mary Poppins?"

Tapping her finger to her nose before pointing to me, she says, "Yes! I knew you looked familiar."

"I don't want to look like a British nanny about to spend the day drinking tea and flying kites," I tell her in a pout.

"Psh, yeah you do. Every little boy on the planet had a thing for Mary Poppins. The men will love you and the woman won't be threatened by you. It's a good look."

I don't have time to worry about it now. I hurry to the bathroom and generously spray on my favorite perfume in hopes of adding to my appeal, before Teisha and I get busy loading up the truck. I keep my serving trays, utensils, and linens in the van because my apartment is too small to store them. Pushing aside a large storage bin, I make room for the coolers and assorted grocery bags.

"How many people is this lunch for anyway?" my friend asks.

"Seventeen," I tell her. "I made enough for twenty-two just in case. You never want to run short, especially on a first impression."

After pulling out onto 34th Street, which is the southernmost tip of the Garment District, we drive through Chelsea, Greenwich Village, Soho, and Tribeca before finally hitting the Financial District. I'm so in the zone that we've gone several blocks before I notice the trees, that only weeks ago were bare, are now full of lush green leaves. Some are adorned with pink and white buds primed to burst into blossoms. It takes us forty-five minutes to go three miles. So, surprisingly fast for New York.

Pulling under the building, I park the van in the loading area by the elevators. With the emergency lights flashing, we unload. Then Teisha stands guard, while I go park.

By the time we're on our way up to the forty-second floor of the Liberty Bank Building, my heart is racing like I just ran a three-minute mile. I'm so nervous I'm sweating. Lifting up an arm, I take a sniff to make sure I'm not stinky.

My friend laughs. "You smell fine. You look fine. Relax, will you? You're acting like you've never had a catering job before."

"I need something steady to come from this if I want to stay in New York. I *need* them to like me."

"Girl, you're the most likable person I've ever met. Of course they're going to like you."

When the elevator finally opens—it takes a long time to climb forty-two floors into the Manhattan skyline—I'm feeling a little better.

A tall and very good-looking man with light brown hair is waiting in the lobby right outside of the elevator. He stands up and greets us, "Which one of you is Aimée?"

He *is* English! I raise my hand as he gushes, "Thank you so much for being so accommodating. My boss would have made me make lunch myself if I couldn't find someone, and I assure you, nobody would have survived that." He winks playfully before adding, "Plus I had a date last night. And while we've just met, I feel comfortable telling you that he let me blow his trumpet."

Teisha bursts out laughing. "That's a euphemism I haven't heard before." Then she sticks out her hand and says, "I'm Teisha."

Byron winks at her. "My date was with a jazz musician, lest you think I was being too loose with my charms."

"Ah, so he let you play his actual trumpet," she says.

He shrugs. "Sure, let's go with that. Now, let's get you moved into the kitchen and then I'll show you the conference room we're using for lunch."

The view walking through the clear glass doors of Fitzwilliam & Associates is very impressive. Sleek furniture, primarily in black leather and chrome, adorns the lobby. The walls are painted a grey so light they almost look silver. The paintings hanging on them are modern splashes of color that probably cost more than I make in a year.

Looking out the window at the Brooklyn Bridge causes me to be momentarily paralyzed as a wall of amazement hits me. *This is the big time, Aimée. Do not screw it up.*

A tall brunette in a pencil skirt so tight it looks painted on, pulls me out of trance by asking, "Who smells?"

I'm about to covertly sniff my armpit again, when she clarifies, "Who dared to wear perfume today?"

Byron looks at her, and shrugs. "That's my bad, Cindy. I forgot to tell Aimée here that WL Senior is severely allergic to scents." Turning to me, he says, "Do you have anything else you can wear? After we get you washed up that is."

"I … I don't," I stutter, horrified to have made such a bad first impression. I always used to keep extra clothes in my van upstate, but I haven't exactly had a run on business since I've been here.

"Oh, for God's sake," Cindy sneers. "I have an extra pair of slacks in my office if you can find her a shirt."

I'm pretty sure Cindy is at least six inches taller than me and at least two sizes smaller. I'm guessing I couldn't even decompose to her size until I'd been dead for a year. There is no way I can wear her pants.

"Go get them," Byron tells her. "Meet me in the boss's office. She can shower in there."

I'm suddenly whisked away to some inner sanctum while leaving Teisha in charge of the food. I could die of mortification.

"Mr. Fitzwilliam will be out for the next hour, so you can use his private bathroom to see to things." He waves his hand in front of me like he's either casting a spell or trying to read my aura. Then he hurries out of the room.

The office is as elegant as an Edwardian gentleman's club in England. I know that from the descriptions in the hundreds of bodice-ripping historical romances I read as a teenager. There's a wide bookshelf (full of books and awards), an enormous mahogany desk, a sitting area including armchairs and a couch, as well as a round table with four dining chairs tucked carefully under it. Everything looks antique and awfully expensive. I'm half-tempted to lie down and roll on the oriental rug to see if it's as soft as it looks.

I cannot imagine being this important. I only hope the short bald man—because *the boss* is always short and bald for some reason—who calls this office his own appreciates how good he has it.

When I open the door to the bathroom, I let out an audible gasp. The shower is as big as my entire bathroom and it looks out onto the East River. Getting naked in here is going to make me feel like I'm on display for the world to see.

I hurriedly pick up my phone and text Teisha.

Me: Are you okay?

Teisha: I've got everything under control. Don't worry about a thing.

Me: Are you wearing any perfume?

Teisha: Nope.

Me: Okay, I'll be out as soon as I can. You would not believe the office I'm in!

Teisha: Pretty flashy, huh?

Me: You could say that.

I slowly start to take my clothes off while hoping that Byron finds a fat woman's pants for me to put on. Once I'm in the shower, I scrub myself as quickly as I can. The soap is an old-fashioned bar of Ivory and I run it all over my body before giving myself a good rinse.

I'm about to step out of the shower when I hear, "For the love of God, Byron, leave me alone. I'm in a hurry."

The voice is right outside the bathroom door! Holy crap, did I lock the door? I step out of the shower in hopes of making sure no one can get in. As soon as my wet foot hits the shiny marble floor I slip and slide across the room like I'm starring in *Frozen on Ice. Let it Go!!!*

As luck would have it, that's the exact moment the door opens, and I fall into the arms of the most devastatingly handsome man it has ever been my pleasure to lay eyes on—thick, dark hair that looks like not even one strand would dare to stray from where he wants it, moss-green eyes with flecks of gold and coffee-colored rims, and—oh, wow—a chiseled manly-man jawline peppered with two-day stubble. I gawk up at him with sheer disbelief. I'm so blinded by his gorgeousness; I'm temporarily rendered mute.

With his arms around me, he calls over his shoulder, "Byron, you left one of your desperate strays in my en suite."

Two things. One, his British accent is so dreamy, it almost makes me want to swoon even though he just tossed out one of the worst insults anyone has thrown my way. And two, he smells so damn good, I want to rub myself all over his neck. Then, of course, there's the other thing. I'm buck naked.

Chapter Four

Noel

I stare at the woman pressed up against me, momentarily mesmerized by the feeling of her warm, wet curves. Her cheeks are flush with what I'm sure is embarrassment, but between the way her mouth is slightly open and her utter lack of clothes, she looks ... well, she looks very much like I imagine she would in the throes of passion. My entire body must think that's what's happening because it has instantly and decidedly reacted in a way that is definitely not suitable for work.

I should let go of her. Now.

Okay ... now. Seriously, arms.

Naked beauty narrows her eyes at me. "Did you just call me a desperate stray?"

Careful to maintain eye contact so she won't think me a pervert (even though, inexplicably, my hands are settled on the curve of her hips and I have a rather obvious physical reaction to her that I hope she won't notice, I say, "I assumed you were with Byron. He tends to collect young women in need of an ego boost."

Byron appears at my left and says, "Oh, she's not mine. She's the caterer." He reaches past me with one hand and holds out a pair of black trousers. "Here you go, love."

She snatches them from Byron, then attempts to cover herself while backing away, leaving my shirt wet and my arms empty. "Do you mind?"

"To be honest, I do," I say, snapping out of the spell I was under and going right back into business mode. "I'm in rather a big rush this morning and I need to shave before my clients get here."

"I didn't … that's not what I meant." She holds the black fabric against her naughty bits while I try not to notice the glorious sight of some very ample side boob, not to mention a shockingly nice view of her round bottom in the mirror behind her.

I force my eyes away from her behind and back to her very lovely face. "Well, for the sake of efficiency, please say what you mean."

Through gritted teeth, she practically growls, "*Please leave* so I can get dressed." *Ah, the naked lady has a temper. I can work with that.*

My cheeks heat up and I nod. "Yes, of course. Obviously that's what you meant."

Byron grabs me by the elbow and yanks me out of the room, shutting the door behind him. "Come on, before you get sued for harassment."

I spin on my heel and give him a 'Well? WTF?' look.

"Right. About that," he says, pointing to the door. "She came in lathered in perfume, but it's all fixed now. Well, nearly." He walks over to my closet where I keep a couple of spare outfits for all-nighters and slides open the door. "She'll need a shirt."

Rubbing the bridge of my nose, I let out a long sigh. "How is this happening, today of all days?"

He pulls a white button-up off its hanger and strides in the direction of the en suite, avoiding eye contact. "Who's to say why life unfolds the way it does? Fate? God? The universe?"

Folding my arms across my damp chest, I say, "*You*, forgetting to tell the caterers not to wear any scents?"

Glaring back at me, he hisses, "Are you honestly going to complain? She is lovely and that was the most action you've seen in months."

Before I can object, he gives the bathroom door three sharp raps. "Aimée, hon. I have a shirt for you. And don't worry, it's me Byron, not my creepy boss."

The lock clicks and the door opens a crack. She sticks her arm out and whispers, "Is he still here?"

Byron leans in and I hear him mutter something that sounds a lot like "unfortunately" before he says, "My god, those pants are tight on you. Can you even breathe?"

Her response isn't audible in spite of the fact that I'm straining my ears. A second later, Byron disappears into the room and locks the door, leaving me waiting to use my loo—emphasis on the *my*— while he attends to the bloody caterer. I tap my foot impatiently, torn between complete irritation and jealousy that my brother is in there instead of me. There are some serious benefits to being Byron—the most obvious is having an all-access pass to women in various states of undress. After a minute, I decide I might as well sit down and look over the presentation again, even though I know there is literally nothing we can add at this point. And even if there were anything that could be improved upon, I'm not exactly capable of coming up with it whilst my brain is so lacking in blood.

I take a deep breath and tell my heart to slow down so I can actually think, but the only thing I end up doing is reliving the moment over again. Her face floods my mind, followed quickly by her soft, feminine form. Good god, she's got curves on curves—the kind a man could lose himself in for days on end.

Stop that, you idiot! You've got more pressing matters at hand than daydreaming about pressing yourself up against her...Ack! I can't seem to shut this off.

Honestly, the timing could not be worse. Tapping my fingers restlessly on my chin, I resolve to push all thoughts of her aside and get my head back in the game. If ever there was a time to stay focused, it is right bloody now.

Finally, the two of them emerge, Byron first, followed by the caterer, who is dressed in extremely tight pants. On top she's wearing my favorite Fred Perry dress shirt that has been knotted at the front to keep her from drowning in it. Sexy, much?

She gives me a very professional, if not embarrassed smile, and says, "I'm Aimée Tompkins, owner of Nibbles and Noshes." She reaches out her right hand for me to shake.

Normally I pride myself on being a gentleman. My instinct is to stand and greet her properly, holding out my hand and asking her if she's all right. But since I'm still in an uncomfortable way, I stay firmly seated behind my desk. Giving her a nod, I do my best not to look interested. "It's imperative that everything go off without a hitch today, Ms. Tompkins. I trust that there won't be any more … issues."

Her cheeks turn red and her eyes turn down to the carpet. "Yes, of course. I'm very sorry about what happened. That's never … I haven't … I don't normally …" Her voice trails off and I have to fight the urge to get up and comfort her. I'm afraid I'm still not ready to move yet.

I give Byron an urgent head nod in her direction. He glares at me, then seems to realize why I'm not behaving like a gentleman and standing up. He mouths, "Oh, gotcha," then loops his arm through hers. "Don't give it a second thought, Aimée. It's already forgotten." He turns to me. "Isn't it, boss?"

"Wiped from my memory," I lie. "Now if you would excuse me, I really do need some privacy and I'm sure you both have much to do."

Chapter Five

Aimée

Is it possible to die from shame? Because if so, I might be experiencing my last few moments on earth. I had to dampen Cindy's pants so they could stretch enough for me to get them on. It didn't work, so I had to run them under the faucet to get them totally wet. That *barely* worked. Now I'm standing in front of the man who could possibly hold my financial freedom in his hands and am being dismissed like I'm—what did he call me, a desperate stray?

Noel Fitzwilliam is a douche. I'm not one to throw vulgar terms around lightly, but this man is going out of his way to make me feel two inches tall. He deserves every nasty word I can come up with, and then some. I'll have to consult Teisha for more. She's a veritable word wizard when she wants to be.

As Byron leads me out of the lion's den to the kitchen, I trip on Cindy's pant legs four times. "Maybe Cindy has some heels we can borrow," Byron suggests, looking concerned for my safety.

Please, no! I want nothing more from that evil woman with the size two pants. As it stands, she would be off my Christmas card list if she'd been a nice person, and you know, I actually send Christmas cards. "I've got heels in my purse," I tell him while hiking up the pant legs like they're a ball gown and I'm about to drop into a deep curtsey.

Byron's last words after showing me the kitchen are, "Let me know if you need anything. *Anything.* I'll be at my desk in front of Mr. Fitzwilliam's office." He looks down at me with such compassion and kindness, I feel like the desperate stray I was moments ago accused of being.

Teisha turns around to greet me and drops the stack of trays in her hands—luckily, they're empty. "Honey," she looks me up and down. "You're going to get a nasty yeast infection wearing pants that tight."

My eyes fill with tears. Not because of the truth she just shot me, but because this day is going so badly, and I need it to go so well. Running toward me, my friend pulls me into her arms and holds on tight. "You got this, girl. Come on, buck up. We'll figure out something together."

With her hands on my upper arms, she pushes me away from her and announces, "I'd bet you a week of tips that skinny-assed Cindy couldn't even fit into those pants."

"You think she purposely gave me tiny pants?" *What would be the point?*

With her eyebrow quirked in a question mark, Teisha answers, "I don't know what her motivation would have been, but she's so cold she could freeze hot lava just by walking by it. I wouldn't put anything past that one."

45

"How's everything going in here?" I ask, desperately needing not to think about the wet pants digging into my lady business.

"Everything is ready to be put on the trays and taken out. I set up a buffet and drink station in the conference room. I figure these corporate types aren't going to want to pass stuff around the table like they're having Sunday dinner at home."

I nod my head in agreement while pulling the heels out of my bag. Maybe an additional four inches will help me feel like the warrior I need to be today, as well as keeping me from doing a header into someone important. I need this tripping to stop.

After spotting a chair in the corner, I sit down to switch out my footwear. Cindy's pants respond to the shifting junk in my trunk and wait for it, the crotch totally gives way. Teisha stares at me like she's witnessing a particularly horrific car accident. "No! What more can happen to you today?" I hope to God she didn't just challenge the universe and hordes of evil spirits are lining up to have a go at me.

Standing up, I offer, "The good news is they're a lot more comfortable now."

"The bad news is your hooch is hanging out."

I look down and sure enough my pink peekaboo undies that I bought on clearance are showing. "What in the fresh hell do I do now?" I demand.

Teisha takes off her apron and hands it to me, "Put this on."

Following her orders, I ask, "What about my butt?"

She grabs my apron off the table and throws the loop over my head so that it's covering my backside. I must look like I'm wearing a sandwich board.

"Perfect!" my friend declares.

"Don't you think people are going to wonder why I'm wearing two aprons and you aren't wearing any?"

"Psh," she releases her breath like a leaky tire. "I highly doubt these folks are even going to see us. We're just the background. But if you're worried, you can stand by the buffet and serve. I'll do all the wandering around refilling drinks and bussing the dirty dishes."

"Thanks, Teish," I tell her, feeling all kinds of love. "You're the best friend a girl could have."

"Damn straight, I am! Now get those shoes on and help me get the food ready."

Turns out Cindy's pants are still too long for me with my heels. Teisha notices and walks out the door shaking her head. When she comes back, she's holding a stapler. "Sit down," she orders.

"You can't staple the hem! You'll ruin the pants."

"Says the woman who just added an air conditioning feature to the booty."

She's got a point. I hold out one leg at a time while T hems the trousers. I'm going to have to offer to pay Cindy back for these things and I know for a fact she didn't buy them at Filene's Basement. The tag said Prada which means replacing them will take all my profits from this lunch, if not more.

By the time I'm finally put together—not unlike Frankenstein's monster—it's go-time. Teisha and I get all the food out and are standing in the corner of the conference room with only seconds to spare before the suits come in.

Noel Fitzwilliam strides in, so full of confidence and style, he looks better than every single man that's ever been cast on *The Bachelor* put together. I hate myself for the moment of appreciation I send his way. He may be the most gorgeous male specimen on the planet, but he's also mean and arrogant and so full of himself he doesn't deserve my admiration.

Yet not an hour ago I was naked in his arms. BIG sigh.

With his hand on the shoulder of an older gentlemen, Noel says, "We have quite a pitch for you today, Walter. I hope you brought your checkbook." The two enjoy a manly chuckle while Noel shoots me a look of pure condescension. If I didn't need this job so much, I'd start firing my fancy baguettes at him like rockets.

Cindy walks in next looking as smug as the viper she is. She doesn't have eyes for anyone but Noel. I could totally see the two of them together. They deserve each other. They would make cruel but ridiculously gorgeous babies who would grow up to be school bullies.

Once everyone is seated at the conference table, Byron comes in and announces, "Our lovely caterers will serve lunch as soon as you're ready."

Noel smiles at him—is it me or do they kind of look alike?—before saying, "Any time, Byron."

Byron hurries over to us. "Okay, girls, you're on. Give them all a little bit of everything."

"I thought we were serving buffet-style," I say, feeling tentacles of raw panic start to grip my insides.

"No, Mr. Fitzwilliam likes to give his clients five-star treatment. Start with the older man and the two people on either side of him, and then Mr. Fitzwilliam. There's no particular order for everyone else."

Teisha and I immediately start plating lunch while I whisper under my breath, "So much for your brilliant plan that would allow me to keep my dignity."

"You stay on the side of the room by the window and I'll take the side with the old guy. That way you can sidestep and look less conspicuous."

While I appreciate her suggestion, I can't imagine I'm going to get through this lunch without one or two people concerned for my sanity. It's true that most people don't pay any attention to catering staff, but that's only when they look normal. When you look like you should be standing on a street corner advertising BOGO corn dogs, it's another story entirely.

After Teisha carries the first three plates out, I grab my one to serve the boss man. *I might just abbreviate that to the big BM for expediency sake.* Noel doesn't even look at me when I serve his lunch, the stuck-up dandy. So much for any chemistry I might have felt while enfolded in his big strong arms. I will never say this out loud, but in my deepest darkest vault of secrets, it will go down as one of the most erotic moments I've ever experienced.

"Ms. Tompkins, are you unwell?"

Noel's voice startles me out of the memory I was apparently reliving publicly. The heat of embarrassment practically devours my face. Instead of answering him, I snap to attention and hurry over to the buffet to get more plates.

Once lunch is served, Teisha and I stand back near the buffet table and watch as the food disappears. Murmurs of "delicious," and "did you try the ...?" are heard around the room, and I grin over at T, momentarily forgetting my double aprons and my stapled, soaked pants. (Not one bite is left on a plate, not even Cindy's.)

The only person who doesn't seem to comment on the food is Noel, who's recently moved so he's sitting next to the older gentleman he walked in with. He's far too absorbed in his conversation to notice anything else. I suddenly realize I'm on pins and needles waiting for him to give me a nod or a smile or say something nice about the food. I shouldn't care what a total jerk like him thinks, but since he is the man in charge, it would at least give me a hint as to whether he might turn into a repeat client.

When the moment is right, Teisha and I clear the plates and napkins. When I take BM's plate, he looks up at me. For a brief second, he smiles and my heart pounds a little, expecting a compliment. Instead, he says, "Please put the cookies on the table, then make your way out."

A sting of humiliation hits me as I wipe the hopeful grin off my face. I'm the help and nothing more. I replace the impulse to give him the finger with a quick nod, then Teisha and I do as we've been told.

I'm just about at the door, my arms loaded with a plastic bin of dirty dishes, when Noel signals for me to come back.

I approach him like I'm sneaking up on a sleeping dragon—with extreme caution. "Ms. Tompkins," he says. "Please don't leave until I have a chance to speak to you."

Oh. My. God. I can just imagine what kind of horrible things he's going to say to me. Words like, unprofessional, incompetent, and inept fill my head like a swarm of killer bees. There is no way. No. Way. I'm going to wait around and take whatever abuse he has in store. No, sir. I'm going to grab my check from Byron and beat it out of here like I just knocked over a bank and the police are after me.

I'm so sure Fitzwilliam & Associates are never going to hire me again, I'm not even going to offer to pay Cindy for her pants. I'm just going to take the money and run.

Chapter Six

Noel

"With that, I'll turn it over to Ali Burman, one of our renowned senior architects, to provide a comprehensive look at the sustainable aspects of the design. We're particularly proud of the double-glass facade he came up with, as well as the rainwater capture system, and the solar panels that will create enough power to substantially lower the electric bills." I give Ali a nod and an encouraging smile.

He gets up and makes his way to the front of the room and stands at the podium next to the screen. I take the opportunity to walk over to the buffet table and pour myself a water, my hand shaking slightly. *It's okay. We're off to a good start. You can relax now.* I use my vantage point at the back of the room to observe Walter Brown Senior. Huh, he doesn't seem all that interested. Instead of being rapt by Ali's explanation of the unprecedented power and heating savings, Walter is sniffing a cookie and turning it over in his hand. He takes a bite, then nods and closes his eyes for a second, lost in whatever's happening in his mouth.

I quietly slip into my spot next to him, hoping it'll refocus his attention, but it's no use. He takes another bite, this time making a low "mmm" sound. Turning to me, he whispers, "Have you tried one of these?"

I shake my head, then glance at Ali in an effort to redirect him, but he misses the cue and picks up a cookie with his meaty fingers. He holds it out to me. "Try it. Best cookie I've ever tasted."

I smile to hide my discomfort with taking food someone else has touched. Who knows when the last time he washed his hands was? I once read that men in positions of power tend to be single-shake, no-wash guys due to the feeling of being in a perpetual hurry. I'm not one of those men, but Walter very well could be. I take a bite of the opposite side that he made contact with. *Mmm, wow.* I'll be damned. He's right. That is the best cookie I've ever tried. It's a gingersnap that appears to have been rolled in sugar before it was baked giving it a crisp outside while keeping the inside soft. The combination melts on my tongue and I suddenly don't care if Walter's a single-shake guy. I'd punch my own brother in the face for one of these.

While I'm savoring the spices as they burst in my mouth, I can't help but think, *of course Aimée makes delectable cookies*—she didn't get those curves from eating apples. Bugger it, now I'm picturing her wearing only an apron, holding out a tray of cookies and smiling at me. The memory of her soft skin against my palms floods my mind and before I know it, I've wolfed down the entire cookie without realizing it (or hearing a thing Ali is saying).

Walter jabs me in the arm. "I was right, wasn't I? Best damn thing I ever put in my mouth."

I nod. "Very much so," I whisper, thinking of all the other things of Aimée's that I could put in my … *Stop it Noel, focus.*

"Can you give your caterer's number to my girl?" he asks, gesturing to a woman three seats over who's furiously taking notes. I wonder how she likes being called his "girl."

I turn my attention back to Ali, but apparently Walter's not done talking about the caterer. He leans in and whispers, "Nice that they hired that mentally handicapped girl, too. My wife is always hassling me to support businesses like that."

"I'm sorry, what?" I say, narrowing my eyes.

"The one with the two aprons. She looks normal but there's got to be something wrong up there," he says, tapping the side of his head. "She stapled her pants, for God's sake."

I blink quickly, trying to determine why his words are bothering me in any way, shape, or form. Nope. No idea. There's no logical reason it should irritate me in the least. And yet … "I'll be sure to pass the number along. Oh, Ali is about to talk about the rain-collection system. You're going to love it."

He snatches a chocolate chip cookie off the tray and sniffs it, and it hits me. Walter Senior isn't the man in charge anymore. He acts like he is, with his blustery presence, but the one making the decisions is definitely his son. I stare at Junior, who's sitting back in his chair with his arms crossed, listening intently. Why didn't I realize it when they came in and their staff jostled for positions next to

Walter Junior? Well, bugger, I've completely ignored *him*. I'll have to right this immediately. The woman sitting next to him leans in and whispers something in his ear. Without taking his eyes off the screen, he nods. Yup. He's the boss.

And I'm going to have to make sure to acknowledge that fact, because if there's anything a child taking over the family business hates, it's having people assume they're only inheriting it because of *who* they are. But this type of thing has to be very delicately done so as not to make it appear that I'm disregarding the man who still fancies himself the head honcho. My palms suddenly feel clammy as I try to figure out how to fix this. I need to have a private conversation with him, but I can't move too fast. There are a surprising number of parallels between bidding on a job and dating. Never give off even a hint of desperation. I quickly jot a note for Walter Junior:

Text me on Tuesday so we can talk business.

212-555-4686

There. A four-day window sends the message that I'm interested but if he doesn't want to go with us, we've got plenty of other real estate developers knocking on our door. Ali finishes to a round of polite applause, and I jump up, suggesting a ten-minute break. Everyone disperses to make phone calls and use the loo, while I make a beeline for Byron. Handing him the note, I lower my voice. "Get this to Walter Junior—and for God's sake, be discreet."

He takes it from me and starts to walk away, but I stop him. "First, go find Ms. Tompkins and have her wrap up any leftover cookies for Walter Senior. Oh, and get one of her business cards for him as well."

The meeting resumes without Byron returning. Cindy's presenting, and for the first time, I notice how painfully thin she is. I find myself wondering if she has an eating disorder. Seeing Aimée in her trousers was rather enlightening. *Dammit, Noel, what is wrong with you today?* Speaking of focus, where is Byron? He must have gotten distracted chatting with Aimée. A moment later, he sneaks in, shutting the door behind him. In one hand, he has a small brown paper bag folded neatly at the top. He gives me a thumbs up that in Byron-speak means he took care of my requests. (Which actually means he likely forgot at least one of the three things I directed him to do.)

He creeps over and kneels down next to me, whispering, "I just caught her on the way out. Her card is in the bag."

"She's gone?" I whisper-yell. *But I told her to stay.* Not that I had a good reason, mind you. In fact, even as I was asking her to wait, I didn't have the first clue what I was going to say to her. *Good job? Nice cookies? I'd like my shirt back, but can you leave it on my bedroom floor in the morning?*

"Don't worry, I gave her a nice, fat tip," he whispers. "Although I can see by the look on your face, you wanted to be the one to do that." His naughty wink has me rolling my eyes. I'm guessing I wasn't too subtle in my admiration for our new caterer and now Byron is probably going to tease me mercilessly about it.

I glare at him and snatch the bag out of his hand, passing it to Walter Senior. Leaning over, I say, "For the road."

He grins at me like a child on Christmas Eve, making me wish he were the man who was about to decide our fate because he's pretty easy to please. But, based on the fact that he's just opened the bag and is now filling it with more cookies from the tray, I'm relatively certain that his days of developing the Manhattan skyline are behind him.

Chapter Seven

Aimée

"**O**pen the envelope," Teisha orders as soon as we get onto the elevator.

"I'll open it in the van. My hands are shaking so badly I need a moment to collect myself."

T makes a grab for it, but I tuck it down my shirt–er, Noel's shirt–before she can get it. "Down, girl. I want to be the one to look, but I just need a minute."

She snags a leftover baguette from the cooler and takes a bite. Then she moans, "Oh my god, this is so good! What's in here?"

"Grilled eggplant, peppers, mushrooms, onions, and goat cheese all marinated in an herbed olive oil, then topped off with a reduced balsamic drizzle."

"This is delicious enough that I don't think anyone is going to even remember the perfume incident." She takes another bite. "Damn, that's good!"

Her reaction makes me feel the tiniest bit better about the godawful start to this job. Who in the history of catering has ever wound up naked in their employer's arms outside of a pornographic film? I suddenly wonder what Noel was planning to say to me had I stayed behind like he ordered me to.

I know I should be thinking of him as Mr. Fitzwilliam, but I'm afraid that ship sailed when I felt his hands grab my bare butt. God that was a great moment. Horrifying yes, but mind-blowingly delectable otherwise.

Teisha has finished her whole sandwich by the time the elevator arrives in the parking garage. Even though it stopped a dozen times to let people on and off, she should not have had time to eat the whole thing. She practically hoovered it.

I grab a sandwich for myself after we get off the elevator and take a bite while I get the van. I'm so happy in this moment that I no longer register the discomfort of Cindy's pants of torture—C-POT for short. Once I reach my destination, I look around to make sure no one is nearby before unknotting Noel's shirt and taking the pants off. Sweet relief is mine. I start to feel the blood circulating again and I decide in this moment I will never go on another job without taking extra clothes with me. Also, I'm going to eat yogurt every day this week to avoid getting the yeast beast T cautioned me about.

Crap! That's when it hits me, I forgot my dress in Noel's bathroom. Well, I obviously can't go back for it. Can I? I pull out the envelope Byron handed me and open it up. Teisha will be mad I didn't do it in front of her, but I suddenly have to know what's in there before another second goes by. Byron and I contracted for thirty dollars a person for lunch plus thirty dollars a person, per hour, for service. I quickly do the mental math and realize the check should be for seven hundred and twenty dollars, as long as they didn't dock me for the shower I took or the pants I ruined.

I close my eyes while I pull out the check before taking the slowest, deepest breath of my life. Then I look. Holy crap! It's made out for eight hundred and seventy dollars! That's a twenty percent tip on a job I practically blew by wearing perfume.

I hurry to pull the van around to where T is standing with our stuff. Jumping out of the driver side looking like I just performed a tawdry walk of shame—I'm wearing four-inch heels, a man's shirt, and nothing else— I shout, "T! We got a hundred and fifty-dollar tip! WOO-HOO!!! Where should we go celebrate?"

She eyes me up and down before replying, "I think we need to get you some clothes before we go anywhere. Also, I told you we nailed that job! Show me the check." She grabs it before I can hand it to her. Peeling a post-it note off the back, she asks, "What's this?"

I take it out of her hands and read:

Text me on Tuesday so we can talk business.

(212) 555-4686

"It must be from Byron," I conclude. "He probably wants his boss's shirt back or something."

Teisha opens the back of the van and starts to load stuff in while saying, "I bet he wants to set up the next luncheon."

"From your mouth to God's ear, my friend. Seriously, if they hire me again, I'll pay Cindy for her pants."

"No, you won't. I'll take them down to Kwan and he'll fix them for you."

I jump into the back of the van to organize the stuff as she hands it up. "Your nail guy is going to fix Cindy's pants?"

"Nah, his cousin Don is. He's a dry cleaner and tailor somewhere around China Town. I take my stuff to Kwan and in a few days he returns it, good as new."

"Only in New York," I tell her.

It takes us an hour and fifteen minutes to get back to midtown. To my right, the wide sidewalk is crowded with women dressed in the latest spring fashions and men who have removed their suit jackets and slung them over their arms. There's also an old lady with a walker who keeps catching up to us every couple of blocks. It's a little disheartening and I'm tempted to go on my regular rant about how Manhattan should just ban all cars and install giant conveyor belts where the streets are. We'd sure get around faster. But I've got bigger problems in front of me than solving the city's traffic woes. We finally pull into the parking garage under my building, a rarity among New York City apartments, but one of the reasons I had to settle for such tiny quarters.

"I'm going to start moving over to your place tomorrow if that works," I tell my friend. "My landlord starts knocking on doors on the third of the month so if I'm out by the second, we won't have to have words."

"You've got my key," she tells me. Then she asks, "Why do you suppose Byron wanted you to wait until Tuesday to text him?"

I shrug my shoulders. "Maybe because he won't have the information for the next lunch he wants us to cater until then."

I shrug my shoulders. "Maybe because he won't have the information for the next lunch he wants us to cater until then."

"Yeah, that's probably it," she agrees. "Darn, because if there were a Tinder to pick friends, I would definitely be swiping right."

"Same. I kind of have a little crush on Byron even though I know it'll never happen."

Teisha nods. "I think we need to bring that boy into the fold, don't you? Now that Terrance is leaving, we need another gay guy around. Who else will remind us that bangs are the calling card of the devil?"

"We are not jumping into a friendship scenario with the man who has the power to make or break my recently resuscitated catering career. Just no. We're going to take it slow and make sure we cement the professional portion of our relationship before we go all gay babe on him."

After we unload the van, Teisha says, "Let's get Chinese. I like to celebrate with a little kung pao."

After putting on yoga pants and a hoodie, I lead the way out of my apartment. T and I walk up to Red Flower on East 54th Street, talking the whole way about what a success we are.

"That boss man was something straight out of *Eye Candy Monthly*, wasn't he?" Teisha asks.

"There's something I need to tell you."

"What?" she demands when I don't speak up quick enough.

"Noel walked in on me when I was getting out of the shower."

Teisha stops walking. She turns to me and demands, "Why didn't you tell me that before now?"

"I just wanted to get through the afternoon without thinking about it."

"Did he see you in your birthday suit?"

I nod my head.

"Did he say anything?" Her voice has practically climbed an octave.

"I actually slipped and fell into his arms."

"NAKED?!"

People nearby stop to stare at us.

"Keep your voice down, T. And yes, he held me while I was naked."

"Why oh why oh why didn't I put on perfume today?" she moans. "That could have been me! I'm going to need details, Aimes, every single little thing you can think of."

I fill her in on what I can remember while she makes sounds like she's at some kind of Baptist revival and is finding Jesus for the first time.

Once we're seated inside the restaurant, she says, "You text Byron right now. Don't wait until Tuesday. We need some intel on that boss of his."

"How in the world am I going to do that?"

"Just start texting him," she orders. "We'll see what he says, and we'll work it out from there."

I pull my phone out of my purse before hitting the message box by his number. Then I type in FitzAssoc to create the contact.

I just wanted to thank you for giving me a chance today. I really appreciated all your help in getting me showered.

Chapter Eight

Noel

I stare at her words, trying to choose an appropriate response. Clearly it's from Aimée who believes she's texting my brother. She would hardly thank me for my part in her shower adventures. It appears likely that Byron gave her the memo meant for Walter Junior, which would be a total Byron thing to do. I make a mental note to contact Junior myself.

Back to Aimée. Obviously, I should tell her who I am. It's not like I want my shirt back—I get a secret thrill thinking of her wearing it. I just don't appreciate her running out on me before I could talk to her. Not to mention I should probably give her dress back to her. (I hung it in my closet, but not before inhaling the lovely perfume that was the cause of much distraction for me today. Whatever that scent is, it's utterly feminine but not at all what I'd call sweet—kind of like her.)

I start to write *I'm not sure how you got my number. This is Noel*, then delete it. Scratching my chin, I find myself grinning. She'd remove the number in a heartbeat if she knew it was me, and I feel like having a little fun. Besides, it's Friday night, and now that our pitch for One Rosenthal is over, I have nothing to do this weekend. After months of working seven days a week, I suddenly find myself with free time.

Muting the sports update I was watching on the telly, I walk over to my kitchen to grab a beer out of the fridge. I twist the cap off and have a long pull on the bottle before glancing down at my mobile. She's waiting for a reply. She left me quite the opening with the whole *I really appreciated all your help in getting me showered.*

How could a guy pass that up? I assign her the very appropriate title of SexyCaterer before typing back.

Me: The pleasure was all mine.

SexyCaterer: Your boss scared the life out of me. Is he always so, so …

Me: Devastatingly handsome? Virile?

SexyCaterer: I was going to say cold and intimidating. He's not the warm fuzzy type, is he?

Me: One can't afford to be warm and fuzzy in this business.

SexyCaterer: Well, most people manage to strike a balance between overly friendly and total a-hole.

A-hole? Ouch.

Me: To be fair, your presence in the bathroom was quite the surprise.

SexyCaterer: I could forgive that part, but the way he acted later—seriously rude. Good thing he has you to make up for his shortcomings. I nicknamed him BM for boss man (and the other way of using those initials together – lol). Anyway, why did you want me to wait until Tuesday to text you? Do you have another job for me?

Hmmm … how to answer that? I should just tell her the truth. I start to type no, but for some unfathomable reason, I can't seem to force myself to press send. Her nude body appears in my mind's eye, and I get lost in the image until my phone dings. I look down to see she's written:

SexyCaterer: Byron, are you there?

Me: Yes. Yup, I'm here. I do have another job for you, but now that I know how you feel about my boss, you might not want it.

SexyCaterer: I've catered for people worse than him and didn't let my personal feelings get in the way of preparing something delicious. Also, I need the work. I wasn't sure handing those flyers out was going to get me anywhere and then you called about today's lunch. Thank you so much for giving me a chance.

Me: Ah, yes, the flyer... Lunch was delicious, by the way. Our guest asked for your business card. Hopefully that will lead to more work for you.

SexyCaterer: That would be great! Now, tell me about this other job you have? Is it another luncheon?

Me: Think bigger. If we land the project we were pitching today, we'll need someone to keep the staff fed for several weeks – morning snacks, lunches, and afternoon nibbles. Even the occasional supper at a moment's notice. There's a team of eighteen people that will be putting in long hours. Can you handle that?

SexyCaterer: Are you serious?

Me: Deadly.

Little does she know, I'm incapable of humor. At least I have been since moving to New York.

SexyCaterer: Then, yes times a thousand and thank you times a million!!!!

Me: Don't thank me yet. We don't have the contract signed.

SexyCaterer: But you'll get it. As much as your boss isn't my cup of tea, he was pretty amazing in there. I could tell the clients were impressed.

Oh, well that's rather nice, isn't it?

Me: Really? How?

SexyCaterer: Every time he spoke, they couldn't seem to tear their eyes away. I saw lots of nodding too, especially from the men. When women do it, it just means they're listening, but when men nod, it means they agree.

Me: Fingers crossed you're right.

SexyCaterer: I'm right.

Me: Maybe it's wishful thinking because if we get the job, so do you ...

SexyCaterer: Maybe, but I doubt it.

Me: I like your confidence.

SexyCaterer: Thank you, but I'm not just saying that for your approval.

Seems like she's just as feisty as I thought. That type can keep a man on his toes.

SexyCaterer: Kidding! I love approval. I just thought that sounded like something a really confident person would say.

I grin at the screen and flop down on my couch, not wanting the conversation to end just yet.

Me: You're funny.

SexyCaterer: Thanks. Not everyone appreciates my sense of humor. Can I ask you a question?

Me: Sure.

SexyCaterer: Why did he call me a desperate stray?

Damn. I was trying to forget about that.

Me: For some reason, Byron attracts single straight women in need of style/dating advice.

SexyCaterer: Yeah, but that was such a crap thing to say—especially to a girl in the buff.

Double damn.

Me: He feels awful about saying that.

SexyCaterer: He should. I have no interest in men right now, even a dreamy one. What I need is a dreamy contract—which you've kindly offered me (sort of).

Dreamy, huh? I wonder if she realizes she wrote that.

Me: I'm glad to be of service. If you ever need help with the other thing … let me know.

SexyCaterer: What other thing? Your boss? As if. I'm too busy trying to pay my bills to add men to my worries.

Me: That bad?

SexyCaterer: Let's put it this way. I'm moving into my best friend's apartment this weekend because I can't afford the shoebox I've been renting.

My gut tightens at the thought of her being in such a bind, and I resolve to find a way to help. Whether we get the contract or not, I can still afford to hire her.

Me: I'll definitely push hard to get you a semi-permanent position at Fitzwilliams. If not, I have lots of contacts. Someone with your talent should be at the top of the catering business. The only catch with working for us is that you have to put up with the boss.

SexyCaterer: For a gig like that, I'll kiss his feet and call him daddy.

That should not have caused my stomach to tighten like that. I mean, I don't really fancy the idea of a woman doing either of those things, but with her…

Me: No need. You'll get an email as soon as we know.

SexyCaterer: Byron, you are seriously the best! I adore you.

Me: Yes, well, I think I might adore you too.

She can *never* find out it was me pretending to be Byron. It would be a total disaster. In fact, I should stop and tell her to email "me" from now on. Yet, that would cut short all of this flirtatious texting, and heaven knows this interchange is the most fun I've had with a woman since, well, since holding the same woman naked in my arms only hours ago.

Chapter Nine

Aimée

Moving over to Teisha's is not as grueling as one might expect. I barely own anything which means I manage the whole relocation in half a day. How sad is that?

When T gets home from work and sees all my stuff, she says, "I totally would have helped you if you could have waited."

"The only thing that was a bit of a struggle was my mattress, but even so, that's only a twin. Terrance helped me bring it up before he left."

T cracks open a Diet Coke and extends the can in front of her. "To good friends, great roommates, and more business than you know what to do with!"

"Hear, hear!" I pick up my bottle of water and offer an air toast. "If I get a contract at Fitzwilliam & Associates, I can give notice at Bean Town."

"When will you hear?" She kicks off her shoes and plops down on the sofa next to me.

"I don't know. Hopefully soon, but I did hear from the company they were pitching the other day. They want me to cater a lunch for them on Monday."

"Monday—as in two days from now? Girl, you're on fire! Do you need me to help with that one?"

I shake my head. "I don't think so. They asked for a buffet because they don't want anyone in the room during the meeting. Probably some top-secret corporate espionage or something." I giggle at my own joke.

"Kwan said to tell you that he'll have Cindy's pants of torture back by Sunday."

"What dry cleaner is open on Sunday?" I ask.

She shrugs. "I'm not sure whether Kwan's cousin really owns a dry cleaner or just a dry-cleaning machine that he stores in his living room. It makes no difference to me where the magic happens."

"I guess I should plan on returning her pants when I'm downtown on Monday. Then I can pick up my dress at the same time."

I reach over to grab my phone off the coffee table and text Byron.

AiméeT: Hey Byron, I need to return Cindy's C-POT and pick up my dress. Can I stop by late Monday afternoon?

FitzAssoc: Cindy's C-POT? That's sounds dirty.

AiméeT: Cindy's pants of torture would be their formal name. That woman needs to eat a cheeseburger.

FitzAssoc: Ah yes, those pants were a little snug on you.

AiméeT: That's an understatement. I split them right down the middle. They're off being repaired now.

FitzAssoc: So that's why you had two aprons on ...

AiméeT: It certainly wasn't because I thought it looked hot. Promise you won't tell her.

FitzAssoc: Mum's the word.

AiméeT: I don't know if you know this, but Cindy has the hots for your boss in the biggest, baddest way.

FitzAssoc: Why would you say that?

AiméeT: Um, because she looks at him like he's a hot fudge sundae and she hasn't eaten in a month—which she probably hasn't.

FitzAssoc: He's a very yummy looking man, don't you think? I bet you wouldn't mind getting a bite of that yourself.

AiméeT: Lol. Never you mind who I'd like to take a bite out of. I should be there Monday, no later than four.

FitzAssoc: I shall long for the moment when I lay eyes on you again.

AiméeT: I'm sure you hear this all the time, Byron, but I wish you were straight.

FitzAssoc: So, you could ravish me and make me your love slave?

AiméeT: Affirmative. Lol. Any news on the contract you were bidding for?

FitzAssoc: Not yet. Why are you coming downtown on Monday? Do you have another job?

AiméeT: With the client you gave my card to!

FitzAssoc: Brilliant. Let me know if you hear anything about us. ;)

FitszAssoc: ...

FitzAssoc: Obviously, I'm kidding.

AiméeT: Obviously. Okay, Gorgeous, I'm off to the market to shop for my next gig. See you soon.

FitzAssoc: All right, you sexy little minx. I've started counting the minutes.

When I put the phone down, I tell Teisha, "I adore that man. He's so funny and easy to talk to."

"They should embroider those words on the gay flag," Teisha laughs.

"You want to go on a field trip with me?"

"That's like asking the folks in my mom's Weight Watchers meeting if they want a brownie. You know I do. Where are we going?"

"I want to check out a new market in the Village. I hear they have all kinds of interesting spices at rock bottom prices."

I quickly pick up my phone again and send Byron another text.

AiméeT: Do you think corporate guys would be down with curry in their chicken salad or would it be better to keep it bland?

FitzAssoc: My personal opinion is that life is too short to eat bland food, so I'd say curry, but within reason. Not everyone is as adventurous as me.

AiméeT: I believe that. Have you ever shopped at Spice-zing! in the Village?

FitzAssoc: I have not. What do they sell?

AiméeT: Um, spices? I'm heading over there now if you want me to pick up some curry for you. I owe you for all your help yesterday.

FitsAssoc: As it would happen, I don't know how to cook, so I'll have to rely on your bringing me a sample of your chicken salad on Monday.

AiméeT: Consider it done, my friend. Later.

T and I get from her apartment on 112th St. to the Spring Street stop on the subway in just under 25 minutes. A horrible thought hits me. Now that I've moved eighty blocks north of my old apartment, it'll probably take me two hours to get to the Financial District for catering jobs. Crap! If I get a steady job with Fitzwilliam & Assoc., I'm going to have quite the haul until I can afford my own apartment again. But that's future Aimée's problem. For now, I shop.

Spice-zing! is a tiny little hole in the wall. If I didn't have the address, we would have totally missed it. There's no sign. As we walk in, it feels like we're entering a secret opium den.

The smells are to die for though. Thick, smokey, earthy, and pungent. Without even looking, I know they have a lot of cumin and coriander. "Hey, dudes," says a young surfer boy-looking guy. You here for the special special?"

"What's a special special?" Teisha demands like he just offered to give her a flu shot with a dirty needle. Her mouth is curled up in a look of horror.

"Special special is today's special spice flavor. You buy one, you get a free matsutake. Gnarly, am I right?" *How is this guy in New York City and not lining up to catch the next wave on a Southern California beach somewhere?*

"You're giving away a free massage when you buy spices?" Teisha grabs my arm. "I don't think this is the place for us, Aimes." She leans in and whispers, "I bet once they get you into the back room, they drug you and sell your ass on the black market."

I roll my eyes at her and ask the proprietor, "Matsutake mushrooms? I can hardly ever find those!"

"Right? It's like the raddest special special ever." I'm guessing someone sparked a doobie before we came in.

"So, no massage ..." T needs confirmation.

"Not unless you want to catch a drink with me tonight." He shrugs his eyebrows flirtatiously.

"Are you even legal?" T asks.

"Totes, mama. Legal as they come."

Good lord.

T cocks her head to the side. "Let's start with the special special and see where that takes us."

My friend is an absolute goddess who does not have a type as far as the men she dates goes. She says finding the perfect man is like finding the perfect pair of shoes—you have to try *a lot* of them on before you find the one you want to wear every weekend. I guess this even means she'll try on a barely-legal surfer dude.

"Can you point me in the direction of your curry selection?" I ask.

He nods his head like it's connected to a windmill and he's trying to create enough power for the lower West Side. "Righteous! Love me some curry."

The backroom is so narrow, we have to stand single file.

T takes one look and says, "No way am I going in there. I'll be out front."

I turn and whisper to her, "Okay, but come look for me if I'm not out in ten minutes."

Shaking her head, Teisha says, "I love you like a sister, but no."

Surfer dude and I continue to squeeze ourselves down the aisle, then he stops suddenly and says, "Dude, you gotta move. The lady here needs her curry."

"Yes, of course."

I can't see who's answering him, but I know that voice. It's deliciously familiar *and* British. "Mr. Fitzwilliam?" I ask, practically choking on the question.

"Yes? Do I know you?" He still can't see me, so he says, "Skippy, can you step aside so I can see who's talking to me?" *This kid's name isn't really Skippy, is it?*

Skippy answers, "Dude, unless you want me to jump up so you can look under me, it's not going to work. We need to evacuate the premises so this bae can get her curry." Then he pushes past me, causing me to do a face plant against an apothecary jar of dried tien-tsin red chiles which knocks over a vial of saffron threads—ooh, saffron threads! Once Skippy's gone, I look up. Yup, there he is, the BM himself, Noel Fitzwilliam, is standing in front of the curry selection in probably the most exotic and off-the-beaten-path shop in all of New York City.

"What are you doing at Spice-Zing!?" I demand, sounding angrier than I'd intended to. "Did Byron tell you I was coming here?"

"Why would Byron tell me that?" He looks as confused as I am. "And how would he even know?"

"Why *are* you here?" I demand again, ignoring his second question.

"Well, Ms. Tompkins, I'm not sure that it's any of your concern, but I'm in the mood for a good curry and I thought I'd make myself one."

"You cook?" The man I met, and by "met" I mean laid naked in his arms, doesn't strike me as a person who knows his way around the stove. A woman's body though …

"Yes, as shocking as that may sound to you, it was the only way I could get decent food at Oxford. Great school. Horrible restaurants." He leans down and practically sniffs my neck before adding, "Now that you know why *I'm* here, would you mind telling me why you're here? You aren't, by any chance, stalking me, are you?"

"As if!" I push him away before thinking better of it. He is, after all, my potential gravy train. "What I mean is, of course I'm not stalking you. I have a luncheon to cater on Monday and I'm making a curried chicken salad."

"Mmmmm," he groans. "Don't forget the raisins. Something spicy always needs a little something sweet to go with it, don't you think?"

My limbs start to feel like they're full of helium and are floating around me. The last time I felt like this was my big Elsa moment in his bathroom. My brain short-circuits and I lose all train of thought, which is why I stand there staring at him in stunned silence.

Chapter Ten

Noel

I shouldn't have come. I told myself to turn around and go home the entire way here, and yet, I completely ignored my good advice. In my defense, I am *unbelievably* bored. Byron went upstate with his new jazz musician to sit in the audience and swoon while he plays at a bar in the Poconos, which means I don't even have him around to annoy me. It's been so long since I've taken a day off work that I don't remember what I used to do when I had free time. I seem to recall playing video games at one point, and I definitely used to frequent the pub with friends back in London, but since I'm no longer a spotty teenager and I haven't had time to make new friends here in the US, I've spent the better part of the day wandering restlessly around my empty apartment. There was literally nothing on the telly that could hold my interest. Not even cricket, which used to be bit of an obsession for me. So, now I'm staring down the barrel of an entire weekend without anything to fill my days (or worse, my nights).

And that's how I convinced myself to make an appearance at this dark little hovel of a spice store.

This is insanely risky because at some point Aimée may very well figure out she's not texting Byron. Then whatever this intriguing feeling is will be—*poof*—gone. No woman in her right mind would take up with a creepy guy pretending to be his own assistant. *So much for being a man of integrity.*

Yet standing in front of this delectable little caterer making vaguely flirty comments about how well spicy goes with sweet is a temptation I cannot seem to resist—even though it makes me feel a bit pervy. Especially now that I'm accusing her of the very thing I'm doing—stalking. *If I were still an altar boy, there would be penance to pay for a sin of this magnitude. Luckily I've let my Anglican membership lapse.*

As soon as the whole spicy/sweet comment flies out of my mouth, Aimée's eyes grow wide and her lips part slightly. The tip of her pink tongue darts out and rests on her top lip like she's really thinking about my suggestion. Good god, she's cute. Seriously adorable. Today she's got her hair up in a ponytail, and she's wearing grey yoga pants and one of those baseball shirts with pink sleeves and a white mesh front. It's a sporty, girl-next-door look that we men generally find irresistible. "Are you all right?" I ask her since she still hasn't answered.

"Yup. I'm good. I don't like raisins," she says with a shrug, turning her head and picking up a tiny vial with three saffron threads inside. She asks, "Why aren't these ever on sale?"

"A couple of centuries ago, they used to be considered as valuable as gold." You don't spend the entirety of your adolescent years studying British history without picking up a random thing or two to impress the ladies. Up until now, I haven't met anyone who would actually care about that little tidbit, which is too bad really, because I can talk up cinnamon like a Sri Lankan farmer.

She nods. "That's why they used to lock the spice cupboards up. No sense tempting the servants with something this dear."

For some inane reason, I lift my hand and run the tip of my finger up and down the tiny vial in her hand like I'm caressing her and not her saffron. Then I decide to one up her knowledge of the spice and wing it. "Too bad about the shortage."

"What shortage?" she demands.

"The shortage that caused the price of saffron to rise to such ridiculous levels."

"Riiight …" she says, putting the vial down. A thin smile crosses her lips, and she glances up at me. "I never did hear what caused that shortage. Did you?"

In for a penny, in for a pound. "A fire. Huge, forest fire. Several really. Jumped the road and took out all the saffron trees," I say, suddenly feeling slightly too warm. "Tragic really. Who knows how long it'll be before they regrow?"

Raising one eyebrow, she says, "Saffron comes from crocus plants."

"Yes, that's what I meant. The fire took out the fields of …" I let my voice trail off, then say, "I'm dying here, aren't I?"

Aimée smiles at me, then covers her mouth. "Beyond resuscitation, I'm afraid."

"I've been working so hard these last months, I must have blown a fuse up there." I point to the general vicinity of my brain.

She lets out a laugh—not a big one, but audible, nonetheless. The sound makes me want to jump on a couch like Tom Cruise did on *Oprah*. Note, I didn't actually watch *Oprah*, I just caught one or two thousand of the replays. Poor wanker.

"Let's hope it comes online soon," she offers.

I've completely lost the thread of this conversation and have no idea what she's talking about. "What's that?"

Narrowing her eyes, she says, "Your *brain*. I hope your brain comes back online soon."

"Oh, right. Yes, that," I say, snapping my fingers. Then, giving her a grave look, I add, "It's not looking good, I'm afraid. The poor thing's been so well-used, it may never be the same."

"Occupational hazard?" she asks, with a look in her eyes that tells me if I keep this up, I may be able to turn this "accidental" meet-up into a drink. Perhaps even dinner. I am so glad I came all the way to this dodgy shop. Well done, me.

"Yes, it happens to architects, especially ones who fly too close to the stars." I shake my head. "Sad, really."

This time she rewards me with a full laugh, the sound even more pleasing to my ears than her gingersnap cookies were to my tongue. "You're smart to be in your chosen line of work. No danger of overusing your brain."

Her smile fades and her head snaps back. "Excuse me?"

Oh, bugger. Why did I say that? "I ... no, I didn't mean—"

She's glaring now. Actually glaring. "To imply catering doesn't take any brainpower whatsoever?"

"Yes, that," I mutter. "Of course it takes mental energy. I just meant you probably didn't have to go to university for six years to get your masters in catering. It's more of a learn on the job thing, isn't it?"

Her face turns red, but unlike yesterday's shower scene, this time, it's with indignation. "So only jobs that you have to go to a university for require intelligence?"

"No, obviously not. Yours requires a lot of skill, I'm sure. There's planning and buying ingredients and putting it all together." *Stop talking, you knobhead. Just stop.* "It's just that you can follow a video on YouTube to make a recipe, whereas designing a skyscraper is something that takes immense skill." So much for stopping.

Yeah, I should not have said that last bit. Her nostrils are flaring right now. They have literally doubled in size. What a cock-up. I've definitely ruined the moment. And it was such a nice one at that.

Aimée raises her eyebrows before saying, "Okay, I'm just going to walk over there so I can mindlessly put things into a basket and take them home. Gosh, I hope there's a good TikTok video for me to watch that will show me how to make a sandwich. Otherwise, I'm going to be in *big* trouble."

She tries to squeeze past me without our bodies touching, but it's impossible in this narrow aisle. I breathe in and am gifted with the same delicious scent on her dress (that I should definitely not have been sniffing like some sicko—twice). My mind goes temporarily blank as I try to salvage the moment. "I … I apologize. I didn't mean to …"

Turning back to me, she snaps, "For both our sakes, just stop. Good luck with your dinner."

I don't think she means that.

"Good luck with your curry." I try to bring the energy of the conversation back to a congenial level. "It'll probably be better without the raisins, actually," I ramble. "I'm sure most people agree with you and don't even like raisins. Just dried-up grapes, really. Properly overrated if you ask me."

But she's already disappeared down the next aisle, leaving me and my dried-up grapes all alone.

Chapter Eleven

Aimée

"What a jackass!" I say for at least the hundredth time since running into Noel at Spice-zing!.

"I seriously love you like a sister," Teisha says, "but I can't take it anymore. You have got to stop complaining about Noel Fitzwilliam. Like right freaking now."

I slam a jar of olives down on the counter and reply, "I'm sorry, but do you remember that guy who asked you to suck his toes? You talked about that for weeks, WEEKS, and I never told you to stop."

T rolls her eyes at me. "If that gorgeous hunk of man, Noel Fitzwilliam, asked me to suck his toes, I'd be on that like white on rice. But Dwayne was no aristocratic British god *and* his feet smelled. His feet smelled and he asked me to suck his toes. Now, I ask you, is that something you would have gotten over right away?"

"He told me it didn't take a brain to be a caterer, T. He insulted the very foundation of who I am!"

"You're a caterer at your very foundation?" Her eyebrow is quirked in such a way as to indicate she's not buying it. "At your *foundation*, you're a lovely human being. You're kind, you're funny, you're charitable. Yes, you are a caterer, but it is not *who* you are."

"Hand me the buffalo mozzarella, will you?" I ask.

"What are you making with it?"

"That caprese salad with the plum tomatoes, Kalamata olives, basil chiffonade and mediterranean vinaigrette." Then, because I don't know when to leave well enough alone, I add, "You know that salad any old monkey at the zoo could throw together."

"Gah! No more!" Teisha throws a kitchen towel at me. "I'm going to work. I'll see you tonight, and for the love of God, woman, Noel can be as big of a butthole as he wants. He's going to launch you into the position of full-time caterer, no-time waitress. Please remind yourself of that."

After Teisha leaves, I hurry to put together the yogurt and cucumber salad before wrapping up the dessert. I made lemon bars and fudge brownies. Lemon and chocolate are one of my favorite combinations. That whole sweet/tart thing sets my tastebuds dancing, unlike Noel's stupid spicy and sweet suggestion, which I *used* to like but never will again. On principal.

Once the van is completely loaded, I run back upstairs to get Cindy's pants and to take one last look in the mirror. After all, it's important to look your best while spending the better part of your day sitting in traffic.

Somewhere around Sixty-Third Street, I start to wonder if there is any way I could pack my stuff efficiently enough that I could manage to take the subway in the future. With my luck, I'd probably be mugged for my goodies and left for dead on the tracks.

By the time I get to my old neighborhood, forty-five minutes has gone by. Damn and double damn.

Brown, Brown, and Green Real Estate Developers is located three blocks north of Fitzwilliam & Associates on Wall Street. By the time I get there and park, I only have an hour to haul everything upstairs and set up lunch service before their meeting.

No one is nicely waiting to take me back to the kitchen like Byron did. In fact, when I walk into the lobby, no one is there at all. It's a typical office, with black leather couches and a tall reception desk under fluorescent lights (but no receptionist). I sit for five minutes waiting for somebody to emerge, but when no one does, I start peeking my head in various offices. While doing this, and coming up dry, I stumble upon the kitchen. I decide I'd better get everything ready to go. *Where is everyone?*

Twenty minutes before I'm supposed to serve—in a room I don't even know the location of— a handsome youngish guy pops his head in. I remember him from Friday's lunch as a two baguette and no salad guy. "Hey, are you Aimée?"

I wipe my hands on a clean kitchen towel and reach out to shake his hand. "I am."

"I'm Walter Brown Junior. We were really impressed by the spread you put out at that meeting over at Fitzwilliam. Thanks for taking our luncheon on such short notice."

"No ... yeah ... I mean, thank you for thinking of me."

He winks. "I've been thinking of your cookies since Friday. My dad even took all the leftovers home with him. He gave me a couple though." Then he says, "Sorry about no one greeting you. We're all back in the conference room brainstorming ideas."

"Sounds painful," I joke.

"You got that right. We've spent years in the planning stages of a new skyscraper that will literally change the way the world views skyscrapers. No pressure, right? Anyway, we're down to deciding between the last couple architectural firms and we get some distressing news that has us questioning the integrity of the design we were leaning toward."

I can't help but wonder if it's Noel's design, but there's no way it would be appropriate for me to ask. Instead, I say, "Better to find out now than after you break ground."

"You're a smart lady, you know that?"

Oh, how I wish I had a recording of him saying that. I'd call Noel and leave that sentence on a loop on his voicemail. "Say, I know this is a crazy question, but would you like to have a drink with me sometime?"

Would I? I think about it for a moment too long, because he says, "I'm sorry if I'm being too forward."

"No, no, no, ... yes," I finally say.

He laughs nervously. "Is that a no or a yes to the drink? I'm a little confused here."

"It was a no, you weren't being too forward, and a yes to the drink," I clarify.

"Just so you know, you could turn me down and we would still hire you. Having a drink with me is not a prerequisite to working for us."

"And because you just said that, I'd love to get to know you better."

He breathes a sigh of relief and offers me another smile. "Okay then, I'll call you in a couple days and we can set something up." He points to the trays on the counter and asks, "Can I help you carry something?"

"No, honestly, that's my job," I tell him.

"I have to show you where the conference room is. You might as well take advantage of a couple extra hands."

I give him the tray with the curry chicken salad croissants while I pick up the salads. "Thank you, Walter. I appreciate your thoughtfulness." Now I wish this whole scene was caught on video so Noel could see how a *real* gentleman behaves.

I'm guessing if I fell into Walter's arms stark naked, he would have hurried to hand me a towel instead of grabbing my butt like he was laying claim to me. *Is it getting hot in here?*

After making sure everything is ready for lunch, I leave the conference room. Walter leans his head out and says, "We should be done in a couple of hours. I'm sorry you have to wait for us to clean up."

"No problem," I tell him. It's not like I'm doing it out of the goodness of my heart. They're paying me to sit around.

After getting back to the kitchen, I tidy up as much as I can before making a fresh pot of coffee and kicking back on a stool. I pull my phone out and text Byron.

AiméeT: Your boss was at Spice-zing! in the Village on Saturday! How crazy is that?

FitzAssoc: Not that crazy. He's a very worldly man, you know.

AiméeT: He's got no game with the ladies.

FitzAssoc: Really? What happened?

AiméeT: He told me you didn't have to be smart to be a caterer.

FitzAssoc: I'm sure he didn't mean it like it sounded.

AiméeT: I'm pretty sure he did. Anyway, it doesn't matter. It's not like I'm dating him or anything.

FitzAssoc: Would you like to? I mean, I could drop a couple hints his way if that's something that would interest you.

AiméeT: No, thanks. I did get a date with Walter Brown Junior though.

FitzAssoc: WHAT?

AiméeT: Impressive, right? The guy talks to me for less than five minutes and he's asking me out for drinks.

FitzAssoc: That's a huge red flag. HUGE. I wouldn't go. He's definitely a player.

AiméeT: I didn't get that vibe from him. I'm pretty sure he's just a nice guy. If anyone's a player, it's your boss.

FitzAssoc: Trust me, he's not a player. He rarely ever dates.

AiméeT: Probably because he tells women how much smarter he is than they are before asking them out.

FitzAssoc: I'm sure he doesn't. Are you still coming by this afternoon?

AiméeT: You bet. I'm bringing you some treats too.

FitzAssoc: Shoot. I'm not going to be here. Mr. Fitzwilliam asked me to do a couple of errands for him and I'll be leaving early today.

AiméeT: No! I was looking forward to laying eyes on your gorgeous self. Don't worry, I'll leave some goodies for you.

FitzAssoc: You're an angel among women. Now, I have to hustle out of here. But before I do, I really think you ought to cancel that date with Walter Junior. Seriously, you deserve better.

AiméeT: Well, until you start playing for the other team, I'm going to have to settle for second best.

FitzAssoc: Let me know what night you're going out so I can light a candle for you.

AiméeT: Lol. Have a good day, my friend. I hope I see you soon.

I spend the next three hours watching Netflix on my phone, waiting for the meeting to end. At four, I finally peer through the window to see what's taking so long.

I catch Walter's eye and he holds up a finger before saying something to the people in the meeting. Then he comes to the door and opens it. "Aimée, I'm so sorry! We're still going strong in here. Why don't you come in and clear so you can get going?"

"Oh, okay, that would be fine, thanks." I make several quick trips back and forth to the kitchen. Every time I come back to the table the room gets so quiet, you'd think I was alone.

When I leave with the last load, Walter slips an envelope into my apron. "I'll call you in a couple of days, okay?" Then he closes the door and goes back to work.

When I finally have everything loaded into the van, I open the check and find the exact amount that we contracted for. No tip. It's not necessarily considered bad form not to tip on a catered event, but it's not exactly classy.

I briefly wonder if Walter Junior is asking me to drinks because he's too cheap to spring for dinner.

God, I hope not. I'm due a decent date after the last few disasters.

By the time I park at the Liberty Bank Building, it's after five. I hope they haven't locked up already. I need someone to let me in so I can drop off Cindy's pants and pick up my dress. I'd text Byron and ask, but I know he's already gone for the day.

Chapter Twelve

Noel

I stand in the quiet of my office, staring into the building across the street. Tiny, cramped cubicles that have been abandoned for the night as their former occupants hurry home to their families. The fading sunlight bounces off the windows, giving them a faint pink glow. I hate this time of day and the emptiness it brings. Most people wish for west-facing houses so they can watch the sunset, but I would much prefer an expansive view to the east. First thing in the morning is when the world is just waking up and the day is filled with potential. It's a lot less lonely then.

I sigh and check my watch. It's nearly five thirty and I'm alone, waiting for Aimée to appear to collect her dress and drop off Cindy's POT, as she put it. I grin at the memory, then, like a punch to the gut, I remember she's agreed to go on a date with Walter Junior. Why that should bother me is anybody's guess. I'm certainly not going to ask her out for two excellent reasons.

First, she totally hates me, as she should after how I've treated her. I must have cringed a thousand times since Saturday night about my YouTube comment. Seriously, I even woke up in the middle of the night last night with my face sore from wincing. If I don't stop soon, I'll have permanent Steve Buscemi-face.

Honestly, there's probably nothing I could have said that would have been more insulting than suggesting she doesn't need a brain for her job. I certainly don't believe that. I just wanted to impress her but ended up hurting her feelings instead. I'm relatively certain there's no coming back from that.

The second reason I can't ask her out is that I'm far too busy to get involved with her—or any woman for that matter. I've tried it before and it always ends with the "you never make time for me, it's like I don't even matter to you" speech. They're not wrong. I'm a terrible boyfriend and I'd make an even worse husband. I'm of the mind that you cannot excel at more than one thing in life, and I've chosen my career over all else. It's the reason I've managed to make it to where I am today at what is considered a very young age in the world of architecture.

Relationships are definitely not for me. I've accepted that I can't have a serious one without either risking my career or being an utterly neglectful family man. As someone who grew up with a selfish ghost of a father, I know how that feels and I'd never put anyone I loved through the same.

I need to set aside whatever these feelings are that I have for Aimée and get back to work. That's who I am, and I'm content with my lot in life.

The hydraulics on the glass doors hiss causing my heart to pick up its pace. She's here. I've spent the better part of the last few hours trying to figure out how to play this, but keep coming up completely blank. Her lovely voice calls out a hello, and I shut my eyes for a second, praying I don't mess things up again. Strolling out of my office to the hall, I do my best to look casual. "Ms. Tompkins, I assume you're here for your dress."

She holds up a dry-cleaning bag. "And to return Cindy's pants. I had them cleaned."

"How very thoughtful of you," I say, noting that she didn't mention the repair work. I stride over and pluck the hanger from her fingertips, letting my skin brush against hers. She stares up at me with those huge blue eyes of hers and swallows before glancing away as though she just remembered how I insulted her.

She reaches into her handbag and pulls out a brown bag. "These are for Byron."

I take them and drop them on his desk, reminding myself not to leave them there unless I want to explain to my brother why the caterer is dropping off treats for him.

She straightens her back, lifts her chin, and announces, "I should get my dress and go so you can get back to your *important* work."

My shoulders drop in reaction to her continued anger. "I really do need to apologize about the other night. It was not my intention to offend you so horribly."

Narrowing her eyes, she tilts her head at me. "So you only meant to offend me a little? Or maybe a medium amount?"

I can't help but grin at her snappy retort, but I quickly get my lips in check. "Not even the tiniest bit, actually, as improbable as that sounds."

"Yeah, it's not exactly easy to believe. But, it really doesn't matter," she says. "Anyway, I'm in a bit of a hurry, so …"

"Right. The dress," I say, gesturing toward my office. "It's in my closet."

I step out of the way so she can go first, then do my best not to look at her bottom while she walks ahead. Okay, so I may have glanced once. Or twice. She stops in front of the sliding grey doors and folds her arms while she waits for me to retrieve her clothing. My heart rises to my throat while I desperately try to think of something clever to say. Something that will fix things. Without looking at her, I confess, "I'm a bit of an idiot, to be honest."

She makes a strange choking sound, before asking, "What?"

I leave her dress hanging and turn to face her. "The people stuff, the whole knowing what to say thing. It's not one of my gifts. Especially around … certain women. I get a bit tongue-tied and tend to say the wrong thing."

Aimée nods. "Clearly."

"You're very talented," I add, grasping at anything to make things better. "You're not just a caterer, you're an artist with a clear passion for your work."

Tugging the dress off the hanger herself, she answers, "It's nothing anyone with WiFi couldn't do."

"That's not true," I say, shaking my head. "You don't just throw things together. You spend your Saturday nights at dingy little spice shops just so you can create the perfect meal for your clients. And your cookies are so good, I've dreamed about them. And I don't even like cookies."

She lets out the tiniest grin and raises her eyebrows in question.

"That sounded dirty, I'm sorry. Obviously I like *those* cookies, just not the dessert cookies."

Then because I haven't dug a big enough hole for myself, I say, "I didn't want you to think I was like Byron and not interested in a *woman's* cookie. Gah, you see? Total idiot! I don't know when to stop talking."

Her cheeks color and she bites her lip, seeming to be trying to decide what to say next. She finally comes out with, "Don't worry about it. I'll still work for you if you need catering in the future."

I'm somehow flooded with relief and disappointment at the same time. "Brilliant. I look forward to it."

She turns toward the door. "I should get going though. I'm parked in a loading zone."

I walk her out, like the gentleman I should have been before. "How did the salad turn out? I assume it was a hit."

She smiles. "Everything went really well."

There's something about her words I find quite alarming. I think she's talking about her upcoming date with Walter Junior. But since I'm not supposed to know about it, I can't exactly talk her out of it, can I? I opt for reminding her of our first moment together, when the heat was undeniably strong. "No naked incidents?" I ask with a devious grin.

Shutting her eyes for a second, she says, "That was a one off, I promise."

"Probably best that way."

There's that laugh again. "I'd say so."

She pushes the button to call the elevator. Much to my chagrin, it opens immediately. After getting on, Aimée gives me a very professional nod. "Have a good night."

"You as well," I answer, wishing I were stepping into the elevator with her. "And I'll have Byron get in touch with you very—" I call as the doors shut in my face.

Smooth, loser. Very smooth.

Chapter Thirteen

Aimée

S tanding in the elevator on the way down to the parking garage, I lay some truth on myself. I did not want to stop talking to Noel; I just had no reason to stay. It's not like he offered me a drink or anything. He just kept talking about cookies. I feel flush at the very thought of it.

Noel Fitzwilliam is a sexy, sexy man, even though he tends toward rudeness with bouts of verbal diarrhea. My phone pings as I pass the twenty-second floor, so I pull it out of my purse and read.

FitzAssoc: Hey, pretty lady. The boss just messaged me and asked if you could come back upstairs for a few minutes. He said he'd pay your parking ticket if you get one.

AiméeT: What does he want?

FitzAssoc: He didn't say, but who knows, it might be work related.

AiméeT: Yeah, okay. I'll go back up. I missed seeing you. I hope his Highness isn't running you ragged.

FitzAssoc: Obviously, he is. But he's such a hunky and lovable guy, I'd do anything for him.

AiméeT: Um, okay.

FitzAssoc: Give him a big wet kiss for me when you see him.

AiméeT: !!!

FitzAssoc: I'm not kidding. It would make the old boy's day. His year actually.

AiméeT: I don't think that would be very professional of me, do you?

FitzAssoc: Sounds like you're not opposed to the idea.

AiméeT: I'm almost back at the office. I'm going to stop talking to you now.

FitzAssoc: Go tap that, girl.

And just like that, the doors open and I'm staring right at Noel Fitzwilliam as he puts his phone in his pocket. He looks up at me with a crooked smile. "Byron said you had something for me."

"What? No!" Byron didn't tell him about his kissing idea, did he? Oh my god, I'm probably beet red. "He said you wanted me to come back up."

"That I did," he confirms. "It occurred to me that even if we don't get the new contract we're bidding for, I'd like to host a Friday lunch for my staff every week. They work hard and I want to let them know how much I appreciate them."

"Really? Every Friday?" I pull out my mental calculator and start crunching numbers. If it's for the same number of people as the lunch I already catered, after paying for food, gas, and other sundries, that weekly meal alone would add nearly two thou to my pocket every month after expenses. Multiply that by twelve, if I can get it to last a full year, mama's going to be back in her own apartment with at least two separate rooms this time. Sure, it'll still be under three hundred square feet, but that's twice the size I was recently in.

"Well then. Would you mind joining me in my office so we can hammer out some of the details?"

"Tonight?" I ask, feeling my mouth go as dry as the Sahara. "Don't you want to go home?"

"Traffic is horrendous this time of day. I prefer to stay at the office late so I'm not sitting in the back of a town car fighting motion sickness."

"You have a driver?" I blurt out. Slick, Aimée. Obviously, he has a driver if he's in the back seat.

"It makes sense for expediency's sake. If I'm not responsible for making my own way to the office, I can fit in a couple extra hours of work every day."

I follow behind him. "Sounds like you work too much."

"I love what I do. There's nowhere else I'd rather be."

"That's sad," I say before I think better of it. I wonder if verbal diarrhea is contagious. I hurry to add, "I'm sorry. That was inappropriate."

Back in his scrumptiously expensive office, he says, "No offense taken. You're not the first person to suggest I have a problem." Then he points to his couch with a thoughtful expression. "Maybe I do. My sofa folds out into a bed in case I want to stay the night. Is that normal?"

He offers me a confused smile, but instead of smiling back, I glance at the couch. Now both of us stand there staring at it silently. I don't know what Noel is thinking, but I'm wondering what that bed looks like pulled out. I shrug out of my cardigan before I get so hot I spontaneously combust. Finally, remembering to answer his question, I say, "I'm sure it's fine as long as you make some time for fun."

Glancing up at the ceiling, he says, "Does work count?"

"Definitely not," I say. "I mean things like going out dancing all night or traveling somewhere exotic. Or … I don't know, going to karaoke with friends—that's always a blast."

"Well, I'm not much of a dancer, I'm afraid, traveling requires a great deal of time, and I'd rather spend the rest of my life washing people's dirty feet than ever singing in public again."

Grinning, I say, "You can't be that bad."

"Oh, but I can."

In response to what I'm assuming is the skeptical look on my face, he explains, "In grade school, I was asked by more than one teacher to refrain from singing in class and was instructed to mouth the words at our annual Christmas concerts."

"No! Those monsters!"

He nods in a most pitiful way and I know he's pretending to be hurt, but there's a hint of truth in his eyes. "True story. I'm scarred for life." He sighs heavily. "Shame, really, because before I found out how awful I was, I fancied myself the next Bono."

I put one hand on my chest. "You poor thing. I can just picture you as a little eight-year-old boy in a school uniform with the shorts and a little crushed heart. What did your parents say when you told them?"

"Never told them. They'd already banned me from singing at home so I knew they'd consider it good solid advice." He rolls his eyes. "Don't embarrass the family by being less than perfect and all that."

A pang of real sadness comes over me, thinking about what crappy parents he must have. "Well, I would have marched right down there and given those teachers a piece of my mind. In fact, if you ever want to sing, I'd be happy to listen."

Oh wow, do I ever want to hug him right now.

He keeps his mock-sad expression going. "I'm afraid it would take years of therapy before I could even sing one bar, but should I ever want to try, you'll be the first to know."

"I'll be here." We stare at each other for a long moment and there's a shift in the air from teasing to truth that makes my skin tingle.

Suddenly, Noel clears his throat. "Why don't we sit down and bandy some ideas about?"

Before I can answer, my stomach growls so loudly you'd think a wild bear had joined us. "I'm so sorry," I apologize. "I didn't eat lunch. I didn't expect the job at Brown, Brown, and Green to run so long."

Noel strides over to his desk and pulls out a bright lime-green box and hands it to me. "Norman Love truffles. I understand they're delightful."

I cautiously take the box like it's full of live grenades or snakes. "You haven't tried them yet?"

"As I mentioned, I'm not much of a dessert guy."

I sit down in the large wingback chair in front of his desk and take the lid off the candy. "That's right, the whole cookie thing." As I pull out a gorgeous heart-shaped red chocolate with a shiny tempered exterior, I add, "They're almost too pretty to eat."

"Hmmm." Noel pulls a stack of menus out of his desk. "I always order dinner in. How does something from Daniel sound?"

"Daniel Boulud's restaurant? Are you serious?" I practically start to hyperventilate. I have always wanted to eat there but have never had the occasion or the money.

"Do you not like it?" he asks, sounding concerned.

"I wouldn't know. I haven't actually eaten there before." As in, I don't have a spare four hundred dollars to blow on one dinner.

He picks up his phone and punches in a number. "Sheldon, this is Noel Fitzwilliam. I'd like to order dinner for two, please." He looks at me and asks, "Any allergies?" I shake my head in awe that he's ordering carry-out from one of the most expensive restaurants in the city as casually as if he were ordering street tacos from a truck.

Noel continues, "We'd like the start with the Coquilles Saint-Jacques and the Poached Chicken Breast with Black Truffle Leg Quenelle. For the entrees, the Red Snapper en Croûte and Braised Legs, Foie Gras with Caramelized Endive." Food is my love language and at this moment, I'm highly, highly aroused. Or in love. I'm not sure I can tell the difference.

"Dessert?" Noel asks, saving me from falling down the rabbit hole of excitement.

"I have cookies," I manage to utter.

"As much as I'd love to eat your cookie, why don't we get dessert as well?" *What did he say?* I decide I couldn't have heard that right and merely nod my head dumbly in response.

"We'll have the Osmanthus Flower Pavlova and the Hazelnut Noisette." He hangs up and announces, "It will be here in about forty minutes. Can you last that long?"

"I'm sure I can," I say while picking up another truffle. This one is bright blue with white polka dots. When I pop it in my mouth, the flavor of wild blueberries bursts onto my tongue. Soooooooo good. "Mmmmmmmmmmmmmm."

Noel is looking at me with something of a shocked expression.

"Are you okay?" I ask, my mouth still full of chocolate goodness.

"Are you? That was an impressive moan." He looks impressed too.

Oh god, I did that out loud? I point to the candy box and say, "You don't know what you're missing."

He stands up and asks, "Would you like a glass of wine?" *He keeps wine in the office?* I feel like I just fell into an episode of *Mad Men*.

"I have to drive home, but I suppose one glass would be nice, thank you."

Noel walks over to a dark cabinet and pulls out two balloon glasses before grabbing a bottle of Beaujolais. "Why don't we sit on the sofa?"

He says sofa, but I hear bed. I watch as he leads the way into the living room set up on the far side of the room. I suddenly feel like I'm on a date. While his back is turned, I covertly sniff a pit to make sure I don't smell. Ew, I kind of do. I've been hauling stuff all day and it's apparently left me less than sweet-smelling.

"Do you mind if I use your bathroom?" I ask, sounding like a pubescent boy whose voice is changing.

"There are fresh towels if you fancy a shower," he says teasingly.

"I think I'll pass on that this time. I don't want you to think you get to see me naked every time I'm in your office." Did I say that out loud?

He turns around and gives me a smoldering look. "That's too bad. I can't think of a better reason to try to lure you in here."

As he opens the wine, I hurry into his bathroom and run the cold water so I can splash some on my face and snap out of it already. I am in Noel Fitzwilliam's office to discuss catering lunches. This is a work meeting. Just because he ordered an expensive meal, is pouring wine, and has recently waxed poetically about my cookies, does not mean that we're on a date.

Does it?

Chapter Fourteen

Noel

What am I doing? Seriously?! The very last thing I should be, that's what. Trying to romance the skirt off the woman I can't stop thinking about, instead of staying focused on work. Ordering a meal that likely costs more than she earns in a week to impress her. Making up Friday appreciation lunches just so I can see her. I don't want to treat my staff to lunch. I mean, do they work hard? Yes. But they're also very well-paid and have killer benefits and medical. I don't bloody well need to feed them too. And yet, I'm going to do just that.

I am pathetic. A total disappointment to myself—first tossing my sense of honesty aside to carry on text conversations with Aimée under false pretenses, then trying to what? Start a relationship I shouldn't be in?

Dammit, Noel, use your head for more than a hat rack.

But it's too late now because I've already started the ball rolling. In about half an hour, an extremely expensive meal is going to show up and the two of us will linger over it while I try not to think about how badly I want to kiss her. And there's *no way* I can kiss her (or do any of the other delicious things that have been rolling through my mind since she first skidded into my arms). I've literally lured her into my lair. If I make even the smallest move in the direction of anything physical, it will make me the worst sort of man—a slimy predator with no intention of a long-term relationship.

I need to back this train up, like now. Grabbing a couple pads of graph paper and two pens, I loosen my tie and sit back down to wait her return. I need to keep this strictly business, so she won't think me some sort of a letch who's trying to take advantage of her. But if she were to make the first move, that would be an entirely different story …

My phone pings and I grab it out of my pocket.

SexyCaterer: Did you tell his Highness I had a big wet kiss for him?

Me: Of course not. But do you?

For God's sake, Noel. Stop this!

SexyCaterer: Tell me the truth. Are you trying to set me up with him?

Me: I'd never do that. Why, does he seem interested?

SexyCaterer: If I didn't know any better, I'd say yes. He asked me to start coming in every Friday to cater a staff lunch, then he ordered dinner for us from Daniel so we can have a work meeting. That's Daniel Bou-freaking-lud's! Do you know how pricey that place is?

Me: I've heard. It definitely sounds like he could be interested in you.

A little squealing sound comes from the other side of the door, and I find myself grinning from ear to ear. She likes me.

SexyCaterer: ...

SexyCaterer: ...

Me: You okay?

SexyCaterer: Yes, good, but let's just say it's been a long day and I'm not exactly spring fresh.

Me: Don't worry about that. He has almost no sense of smell. Plus, he's a gentleman. He would never make a move without knowing with 100% certainty it will be enthusiastically received. And at that point, he's not going to care how you smell.

SexyCaterer: Good to know. Okay, I should go back out there. I've been in his bathroom for a while now and he's probably wondering what's taking so long.

Me: Let him wait. It'll make you seem more unattainable. All men love that.

SexyCaterer: But not potential employers, which is essentially what he is.

Me: Po-tay-to, po-tah-to ...

I slip my phone back in the pocket of my trousers as soon as I hear the lock click. Aimée comes out and offers me a polite smile as she crosses the room. "That's better."

"All set?"

"Absolutely," she says, sitting down on the tan leather armchair that sits perpendicular to the sofa.

I'm on the cushion closest to the chair, which means our knees are only a few inches apart. "I got you a pad and pen in case you want to take notes."

"Oh, thanks." She reaches for them at the same time I make a move to hand them to her. Our fingers touch again, and we both laugh awkwardly. I say, "sorry," at the same time she says, "I've got it."

I pick up my own pad and jot Catering Meeting along with the date on top. "I know I sprang this whole thing on you, so no pressure to start pitching full menus or anything. I thought it would just be a good opportunity to discuss expectations and toss some ideas around."

"Sure," she says with a nod. "Let's start with the basics. How many people will I be feeding?"

"There are a total of forty-two employees including me."

"Wow, that's a lot of people to be responsible for."

"It is," I say, nodding.

"That must feel like a lot of pressure."

It is. It really, really is. Shrugging, I say, "It's nothing I can't handle. I already have a fully staffed firm in London with eighty-nine employees. The trick is to stay focused, treat your staff and clients well, and work your arse off at all times."

She laughs, then puts on a falsely modest tone. "Oh, but it's nothing really …"

I offer a conciliatory nod. "It can be a lot. Luckily, I have broad shoulders."

"But still … you must have to keep so many balls in the air in order to make sure the money's always flowing in."

"Yes," I say with a smirk. "Big ones."

She blushes and shuts her eyes. "Why is it everything I say around you sounds dirty?"

I glance at her full lips. "I have no idea, but I don't mind as much as you might think."

Her face turns a slightly darker shade of pink and she quickly looks down at her paper. "Okay, so forty-two people. I'd need a list of allergies so I can make sure I accommodate them."

"I'll have Byron get you the answer to that." I jot down, *allergies*. Yes, this seems convincingly like a real meeting.

"Great. Any special preferences?" She glances up and our eyes lock.

"No, I trust you. It's not a sit-down thing like our pitch the other day. I'll just have you set up a buffet in the kitchen and keep it open for an hour or so. That way everyone can eat according to their own schedule." I stare at her longer than is typically considered polite.

She swallows hard, before asking, "Any preferences as a fellow foodie? Speaking of which, how was your curry the other night? Did it turn out?"

She means the one I pretended I was going to make. The one I ordered was delicious. Nodding, I say, "Umm, I doubt it would have impressed you."

"Too many dried-up old grapes?" she asks with a playful grin.

I let out a laugh, then nod. "Something like that."

"I'll make sure I go easy on the raisins then. There is such a thing as too sweet." She stares at me in a way that I hope means what I think it means. In response, I give her a lingering gaze that effectively jolts her out of whatever mood she might have been getting into. "What about theme lunches once a month? Sort of an around-the-world tour?"

"Brilliant!" I answer. "I love that idea. Just not Scotland. What they call food is an abomination."

Laughing, Aimée writes something down and says, "No haggis."

"And no deep-fried Snickers bars either," I say with an overly dramatic shiver.

Grinning, she asks, "Have you never tried one?"

I shake my head.

"Right, you're not a dessert guy. Well, take it from someone who can't get enough sweets, they're like deep-fried sin."

"I don't mind a little sin," I say, the air thick with my true meaning.

She reaches down and picks up her wine glass, then guzzles back a surprising amount in one go.

"Thirsty?" I ask.

"Yup," she squeaks out. "Okay, so what's your budget?"

"Oh, well, I haven't thought about that. Should we say midrange? Something that says, 'I appreciate you' without breaking the bank?"

"So, no saffron threads."

"Absolutely not. They're fine people, but I do have a bottom line to consider."

The glass doors open and a man calls out, "Delivery for Noel Fitzwilliam."

I wave him into my office. After I sign for our meals, he hands over the bags, and leaves us alone again. The heavenly scent of our dinner fills the room, adding a new layer of temptation to an atmosphere already thick with it.

Turning to Aimée, I hold up the bags. "Should we eat at the table?"

"Sure." She gets up, grabs the wine glasses and the bottle, and makes her way over to the table while I pull the containers out of the bags. After a minute, we're sitting down to what would be a decidedly romantic dinner for two if it weren't supposed to be a meeting. Who needs a tablecloth, candles, and music when the most enticing woman you've ever met is sharing supper with you?

We eat in silence for several minutes, with the exception of the moans of pleasure coming from my companion. She really has to stop doing that or I won't be able to stand up without spokes-modeling the sham reason we're eating together. I shift in my chair and top up our wine glasses.

"Oh, I really shouldn't," she says, then she bites her bottom lip. "Well, maybe just half a glass."

"Don't worry. I won't let you leave here intoxicated. If need be, you can always sleep it off," I say, sounding like one of the Brotherhood of British Scouts, of which I was once a member.

Aimée glances at the sofa and interrupts my borderline erotic thoughts by saying, "That wouldn't exactly be very professional of me, would it?"

Or safe, I think while slicing into my flakey snapper and having a bite.

When I glance up at Aimée, she's got her eyes shut and she's chewing like it's the single greatest thing she's ever tasted.

"Are you enjoying your food?"

"So good ..." she says with a sigh that could only be described as highly suggestive. "Do you eat like this all the time?"

"No, I usually stick with more somber fare—grilled salmon, brown rice, veggies. That sort of thing."

"That's how you got that body," she says, then her eyes grow wide and she sputters a bit. "Sorry, I did not mean to say that."

I do my best to look scandalized. "Ms. Tompkins, I am shocked. Are you objectifying me?"

"No! I would never want to make you feel uncomfortable," she says quickly. "I mean you do have a tremendously hard body. Not that I've been staring or anything. It's just when ... last week ... in the bathroom … your arms and chest … and … nothing." She grabs for her glass and tips it back.

"Relax," I say with a grin. "I really don't mind hearing about my tremendously hard body. Especially from someone as lovely as you."

She swallows, looking temporarily stricken. "As lovely as me?"

Don't say it, Noel. Just get this meeting back into the safe zone. "Beautiful, smart, fun, amazing in the kitchen …"

"Oh, yeah, I'm the whole package," she says with a roll of her eyes.

Sitting back in my chair, I lower my tone. "Don't do that."

"Don't do what?"

"Don't put yourself down like that. You're an extraordinary woman. Any man would be lucky to call you his."

Chapter Fifteen

Aimée

Noel just called me beautiful, smart, and fun. Oh, and amazing in the kitchen. My blood feels hot and thick like maple syrup being poured over a stack on hotcakes. My insides are quivering in a similar kind of anticipation. How do I respond to a comment like that? I know what I want to do, but jumping into his lap and attaching myself to him like a barnacle on the bottom of a boat might scare him away. Also, what if he's not really flirting with me and I'm making this all up? *Desperate stray, party of one* ...

"Aimée? Did you hear me?"

I look up from my plate and stare at him like he's another species entirely. "Thank you," I tell him sincerely, while trying to hold back a wall of emotion that's building in my brain.

"Thank you for asking if you want more wine?" he looks confused.

"Did you ask me that? I'm sorry, I guess I was wool-gathering." I push my glass toward him and say, "More wine would be nice." I need another glass of wine like I need to gain ten pounds of cookie weight, but if I'm drinking, then at least I'm not talking. That's solid reasoning, right?

Noel opens another bottle and brings it back to the table. "When I was a boy, I used to think I wanted to grow up and be a refuse collector," he tells me.

A giggle pops out of me before I can stop it. "Why?"

"Because our refuse collector was such a happy man. He always waved to people and wished them a good day. I thought it was his job that made him so happy."

"That's sweet," I say. "What did your parents say when you told them about your ambitions?"

He releases a pent-up breath before answering, "My mother cried, and my father threatened to disown me." Then he says, "They weren't overly fond of me becoming an architect either, but they didn't fight me too hard. Probably afraid I'd make good on my childhood aspirations if they pushed."

"What did they want you to do?" I ask, feeling oddly protective of Noel, the boy.

"Get into politics. That's where the real power is. And it's one of the only suitable professions for the son of a lord."

"Oh … I see." I reach across the table to take his hand in mine. I don't know what to say to him, but darn if he doesn't seem like he could use some comfort. I finally go with, "It's hard when people have preconceived ideas about you, isn't it?" I quickly let go, afraid I'm going to give him the wrong impression. Aaaaaaand sip.

"You sound like you have some experience with that."

"Not with my parents, no. They're totally supportive and encouraging of my dreams. I mean, they were hoping I'd be happy making my mark in the catering world back home in Rochester, but otherwise, they're always in my corner." I pause for a second, then add, "It's just, I guess I feel that sometimes in relationships with men—the preconceived notions thing." Why did I go down this alley again? Sip, sip.

"How do you mean?"

I really, really, super really don't want to talk about this, but I opened the door, and the wine has loosened my tongue. Before I can stop myself, I say, "Men sometimes think that because I'm in the service industry, I'm easy." I inwardly pray for a hole to open in the floor and swallow me.

"How so?" He asks.

"Take the guy I went out with last week. He took me out to dinner—appetizers really—and he talked about himself the whole time. Then when we got into the cab afterward, he told the driver *his* address, not mine. When I said I wasn't going home with him, he told the cabbie to pull over and drop me off on the street."

"I hope you kneed him in the jolly roger on your way out."

I love how angry he is on my behalf.

I take another fortifying gulp of wine. Or two. Okay, three. "I wish I had. I did tell him that only letting your date order an appetizer was like advertising you weren't packing anything substantial in the junkular region."

Noel lifts his wine glass in the air and shouts, "Hear, hear!" Then he asks, "But I don't understand what that man's idiocy has to do with your employment. Maybe he was just a total cad."

I shake my head. "I don't think so. Guys who ask you out when you're serving them tend to think they won't have to work too hard to get you into bed. That happens to a lot of us."

"That's despicable." Noel suddenly sits up straighter and tightens his tie. "And maybe I'm not much better than the rest of them. I feel that I owe you an apology. You must think I'm horrible for inviting you into my office for supper. After hours, even." He starts to nervously tidy up the table.

"I don't think badly of you at all," I declare. Then I fling my hand through the air like I'm tossing a baseball. Poorly. "Thish is handsh down the best meal I've had in years and you haven't once made a move on me." More's the pity.

"Yes, well, I held you naked in my arms and that certainly must have given you a moment for pause." Beads of sweat pop up on Noel's forehead and he loosens his tie once again.

"That was an unexshpected comedy of errors. How can you feel responsible when you didn't even know I was there?" Siiiiiiiiiiiiiiiiiiiiip.

"I'm afraid I held on a bit too long," he confesses, like I'm his childhood priest. "And before you excuse my behavior, you should know that I liked it."

"I'll take that as a compliment," I tell him, suddenly feeling the effects of three plus glasses of wine. My heads spins and my stomach bucks. It's like I've just come off the Darian Lake Ride of Steel rollercoaster—the only rollercoaster I've ever vomited on.

"You look a little peaked. Do you think you might need to lie down for a minute?"

"Please." I kick off my shoes and stand up which causes me to stagger. Oh, boy, I think I'm drunk. This meal is the first food I've had since my half bagel at breakfast and whoaaaaaa! the wine got to me before the food could do its job and soak it up.

Noel leads me to the couch and hangs onto my hands while I drop my butt onto the cushion. "Thissssshish nice, thanks."

"Would you like a blanket? I have one in my closet."

"Totally. I would totally, totally, totally like a blanket. Toooooootally."

Noel hurries across the room and comes back with a beautiful silver-grey throw. He hands it to me, and I rub it all over my face. Sooooo soft. "Shmeer?" I ask him.

"I'm sorry, what?" God he's good looking, all British with his black hair and grassy green eyes. Eyes I could roll in ... wait, how would that work?

"Shmeer, shmeer, cashmeere ..." My lips feel funny. Kind of tingly and numb at the same time.

"Cashmere! Yes," he says. "It's a cashmere blanket."

"Wanna sit down with me?" I ask. "You're such a nice man."

"Um, well, I don't know. I don't want you to think I'm getting inappropriate."

"Nah, sit down!" I slap the spot next to me with authority. Once he's situated, I lean to the side and lie down, placing my feet on top of him. "Wanna rub my feet?" I ask. I love having my feet rubbed. So much so that if a strange man with a foot fetish asked if he could rub my feet, I'd totally let him. TOTALLY.

"Aimée," Noel starts to say. He's not rubbing though, so I kick my feet at him to give him the idea. He gently takes my foot in his hands. "I think you might be a little tipsy."

I shake my head back and forth so wildly; I can feel my supper start to rebel. "Not tipsy," I tell him. "I'm drunk. I don't drink a lot and when I do it'sh never more than a glass."

"Oh, I see." He looks like he's about to stand up, so I dig my heels into his lap and order, "Rub."

"This is just … rather … I think maybe I should take you home."

"Why? You gotta bed right here." I pat the couch sharply like I'm trying to kill bugs. "Don't wanna go," I tell him as I pull the blanket up and roll over. "Can't walk when I'm drunk. I jus' need a little nap."

"I don't know. I think I should really help you home." He's a persistent bugger.

"You could but I don't remember my shtreet number."

"Surely you know what your apartment building looks like." He's rubbing my feet in earnest now.

"Ooooooh, yeah, right there," I moan loudly. "That's shoooooo good."

My brain is kind of floating in the clouds and I'm not sure who he's talking to, but he says, "Down, boy!" Does he have a dog?

"Wanna rub my back?" I ask while sitting up. I decide it will be easier for him to rub my back if my shirt isn't on. That, of course, is why I try to take my shirt off. Unfortunately, the motion of sitting up too quickly makes me woozy all over again and the next thing I know …

Chapter Sixteen

Noel

"Oh dear, you appear to be caught in your shirt," I say, trying to avert my eyes while her arms dangle above her head and her—oh wow, that is an unbelievably sexy bra. It's lacy and pink and really doesn't leave much to the imagination. I'm temporarily frozen, just gawking until my frontal lobe kicks in and I realize she needs help.

"I can't shhee!" she slurs. "Itsablackout."

"Don't panic. I can fix it." Reaching up, I take hold of the bottom of her shirt and do the very last thing I want to—tug it back into place. I should be up for sainthood for this.

Her face is beet red and slightly damp. "Oh, that's better. Thanks, sexy ..." she says, running her fingers over my nose and mouth in a way that I'm sure she thinks is alluring but is actually kind of rough and awkward. "Look at you," she whispers. "You are ... like the hottest man ever. Wow."

"Well, thank you."

She runs both her arms up her sides and straight into the air. "Let's do this, mmkay ..."

Weaving a little, she tries to focus on my pants, reaching for my belt buckle. I quickly stand so I'm out of the danger zone. Aimée gives me a pouty look. "Where are you going? I thought you liked me."

"I do. Very much, which is why I am absolutely going to get you home safely rather than taking advantage of you in your current condition."

She stands and drapes her arms over my shoulders. "It's snot takin' advantage if I'm up for it."

"Yes, yes, it would be and only the worst sort of man does something like that." I gently remove her arms from my neck and sit her back down on the sofa. She snuggles into the blanket and closes her eyes with a dreamy smile. "Schmeer's nice too."

A second later, she's out cold. Oh, bollocks. Now what do I do with her? I carefully position her on her side, then cover her with the blanket. She lets out a snore so loud, I wince. Yikes. I hope that wouldn't be an every night thing. But even if it is, I could invest in ear plugs.

What am I talking about? You're not going to have a relationship with her. Do you hear that Noel? No Relationship.

Okay, now to tackle the problem at hand. I have a passed out drunk woman who has a van parked in a loading zone on my hands. I have no idea what her van looks like or where she lives. Glancing around for ideas, I spot her purse. That bag holds the answers. I quickly stride over to it and dig around for her cell phone. Huh, so this is what women keep in these things—there's two tubes of lipstick and some other cosmetic-type items I can't identify, plus lady products, crumpled up tissues, a wad of receipts, gum, mints, *and* saffron threads? I'm suddenly more pleased than I should be that she treated herself. Finally, I come across her mobile at the very bottom of the bag. I swipe the screen. Bloody hell. Facial recognition. Let's hope it works with her eyes closed.

It takes three attempts for me to get into her phone. Then I scroll through texts looking for the last person she's been in touch with. Me as Byron. Okay, second to last is someone named T-bag. This feels like such a violation, but I call the number anyway. A couple of rings later, a woman answers. "Did you do him? Tell me you did him and it was ah-maz-ing. I've heard those stiff Brits can really turn up the heat between the sheets."

Ah, she's been talking about me. I smirk a little to myself, then say, "Umm, hello, this is Noel Fitzwilliam calling. Is this T-bag?"

"It's Teisha. Only Aimée gets away with calling me that," she answers. "Wait. Why are you calling? Did something happen to Aimée?"

"Aimée's fine. She's here with me at my office, but I'm afraid she's had a little too much to drink and she's ... gone to sleep without providing me with her address. Might you know where she lives so I can get her home?"

"She lives with me," Teisha answers, sounding like she's ready to jump through the phone and murder me. "Did you roofie her? Because I swear to all that is holy, I will end you if you roofied her."

"No! Of course not," I say. "I would never do such a thing. We had a business dinner and she had three or four glasses of wine, give or take. Then she passed out."

"Oh yeah, she's a real lightweight when it comes to booze," Teisha says.

"Apparently so," I say, rubbing the back of my neck while I watch her sleep. Not in a creepy way, more in an "oh she's lovely" way. "Listen, I'd really like to bring her home and do something about her van. Can you give me the address?"

"Sure, but she doesn't park that thing here. She's got a temporary spot up in the Bronx."

Bugger. "Okay, I'll find suitable overnight parking down here and then bring her to you."

Teisha gives me her address, describes the van (old, rickety, and white with the words Nibbles and Noshes on the side), then we ring off. I go over to my desk, grab the wastepaper basket and take it over to Aimée. Setting it down in front of her, I say, "Aimée. Wake up, okay?"

She grunts and shifts a little but doesn't open her eyes.

"Aimée," I say a little louder, gently shaking her shoulder. "I'm going to go move your van. I'll be back in a few minutes to get you. Just stay on your side, okay? And if you need to vomit, I have a bin right here."

She nods and murmurs, "Sure bin soft."

It takes me close to thirty minutes to find an overnight parking stall that looks as though the van will still be there by morning, during which time I come close to causing three separate accidents by veering to the wrong side of the road. Well, the right side, if you ask me, but that's beside the point, there were several near misses.

My knuckles are pure white by the time I step out of the beastly thing, and I need Google maps to help me find my way back because I've circled around so many times, I'm completely lost. Great. It's a ten-minute walk back to the office and it's starting to spit rain. I'm about two minutes from my office when a loud clap of thunder bounces off the buildings and the sky opens up, dumping everything it's got on me. When I finally reach the lobby, I'm drenched through. Even my socks are saturated. Lovely. Just how I hoped this evening would turn out.

By the time the elevator whisks me up to the forty-second floor, I'm in a bit of a panic after having left Aimée for so long. What if she woke up and tried to find me and got lost? Or she started to vomit but she was on her back and she choked? So many possibilities roll through my mind that by the time I see her peacefully asleep on my sofa, I'm the tiniest bit angry at her for being fine, which makes no sense at all.

I call for a town car, then grab some dry clothes out of the closet and turn my back on her while I quickly change. I don't bother to go into the bathroom. She's sound asleep, and besides, this way I can keep an ear out for her in case she needs me.

"Oh, yay," I hear from behind me. "Are we doing this? Comeon over, shailor."

"No, no, no," I answer, yanking up my jeans and turning to her. "I already called a car and found out where you live. Teisha is expecting you, so we have to go."

"Okay," she says, nodding, then closing her eyes. "Just let me shleep for a minute. Then we'll go." She drops back onto the couch and her head lolls to the side.

Sighing, I finish dressing, grab my wallet, keys, and phone, stuffing them into my suit jacket pocket. Then I gather her purse, sling it over my shoulder, and pick her up, fireman-style. She makes a 'wee' sound and I say, "Just tell me if you're going to vomit, okay?"

"Sure thing, schmexy."

And so, I spend the entire elevator ride being groped on my buttocks by the woman I'm carrying who I can't do anything with. Pretty great evening all around, really.

Once we're nestled in the back of the town car, I have the driver turn up the heat, and Aimée snuggles into the crook of my neck and sighs happily. "You shmell like a man."

"Thank you?" I think.

"It'shnice," she says. "You're not who I thought you were. You're not a cold a-hole. You're a true gentleman."

I turn my head toward her and inhale the scent of her hair. God, how could someone smell so heavenly?

"I could fall in love with you, you know," she murmurs. "I practically did when you were holding me that first day after showering in your office. Or maybe I did. Does that sound crazy?"

"No," I say, and oddly enough it's true. "It doesn't sound crazy at all."

Chapter Seventeen

Aimée

I wake up staring at a water spot on Teisha's bedroom ceiling, wondering a variety of things. Least of which is, who in the hell is playing drums? I force my eyes closed again and throw a pillow over my head, causing the hectic rhythm to lessen slightly. That's when it hits me. Those aren't drums, that's my heart pounding and blood shooting through my extremities. *Hurts. Hurts so bad.*

"Well?" my friend yells at me so loudly I'm pretty sure she's using a Mr. Microphone.

"Stooooooooooooooop yelling," I hiss. "Head hurts."

"I'm not surprised. I understand you had yourself a little too much to drink last night." That's either judgment or approval in her voice. With T it could go either way.

"What day is it?" I ask, sounding like I'm begging for last rites.

"It's Tuesday. Now wake up and tell me what happened last night."

My brain is so foggy that I have to go through a series of mental exercises to figure out what day yesterday was. Counting on my fingers, which are currently wrapped around my head to quiet the pounding, I mentally recite, *"Monday, Tuesday, Wednesday Thursday, Friday, Saturday, Sunday, Monday, Tuesday. Monday, Tuesday."*

Okay, I'm on fire now. Yesterday was Monday which means I catered a lunch at Brown, Brown, and Green. What happened there? Walter Brown Junior asked me out. Please say I didn't go out and get drunk with him. How unprofessional!

No, wait. I remember leaving that building and driving over to Fitzwilliam & Associates. Yup, there I am returning Cindy's pants. There I am getting my dress from Noel's office. Then I'm eating the most delicious meal that has ever crossed my lips. I'm drinking wine. So much wine. And oh, no, please let that not be me. In my mind's eye, I see someone who looks a lot like me propositioning Noel.

And he's passing on the invitation.

"Oh, my god, T, I got drunk and threw myself at Noel, but he didn't go for it." Humiliation rages through me like food poisoning.

"That gorgeous hunk of man called me to find out where you lived, and he brought you home. That's a class act right there."

"It's Tuesday! It's street sweeping day which means my van has been towed!" I sit up so quickly I have to hold onto the sides of the mattress like a white-water raft to keep from being hurled into the abyss.

"Good lord, you're a lightweight. And don't worry, the King found a parking space for your van downtown, so it hasn't been towed."

"The King?" I squeak.

"I think that's what we should call him from now on. He's got the bearing of royalty about him. I, for one, wouldn't mind being his loyal subject." A little shiver of what appears to be delight runs through her.

While I wait for her moment to pass, I say, "T, he offered me a weekly luncheon for forty-two people! But now there's no way I can take the job. Things were said. Things I should have never even thought."

"Oh, psh. Any man who's willing to park your van and carry your sorry ass home without molesting you first isn't going to judge you for getting drunk. He didn't take advantage of you, did he?"

"Not for my lack of trying." I see myself petting him and rubbing up against him, and—please, say it isn't so—grabbing the buckle on his pants. Oh, the shame. I can never, ever, ever see Noel Fitzwilliam again.

While I'm bemoaning the loss of a fabulous future gig as well as a potential English hottie, the buzzer rings in the living room. Loudly. Teisha yells, "COMING!" which does no good because she has to press the buzzer to be heard by the person who's currently several flights down.

I hear T ask, "Who is it?"

A disembodied voice mumbles something, and then there's a high pitch buzzing and then finally peace until the doorbell rings. There are mumbled voices and an exclamation of excitement on T's end and then nothing.

Moments later she comes into the room carrying a paper bag with handles. "You will never believe who that was!"

"Dr. Kevorkian here to help me pass pleasantly into the next life?" If it wasn't him, I don't care who it was. I can still feel the pain of that buzzer in my temple like I got stabbed.

"That was a delivery dude bringing you breakfast."

"What? Did I order breakfast to be delivered before I passed out?" To be honest, it kind of sounds like me. I like my food enough to anticipate my next meal.

Teisha clears her throat and opens a piece of paper before reading:

Good morning, Aimée,

I hope you slept well. I thought you might benefit from the healing effects of a full-English this morning. Take care and let me know when you want to pick up your van.

Noel

Noel sent me breakfast? He's a god among men! The aroma coming from that bag is causing my stomach to stand up and cheer. T drops the bag next to the mattress and says, "I'll go get forks."

By the time she's back, I have no fewer than six different containers open. There's bacon, scrambled eggs, toast, fried potatoes, grilled tomatoes, sausage, and baked beans. T hands me a fork and two aspirin while saying, "I put a fresh pot of coffee on." Then she sits down and digs in with me. There's easily enough food for four people here.

"I think you ought to marry the guy," T announces between bites.

"I can never face him again, T. I was outrageous last night." Bite, chew, swallow. "I was thinking that maybe you could pick up my van for me."

Shaking her head, she answers, "Not if you paid me a million bucks. Well, okay, I'd do it for a cool mil, but you don't have that, so it's on you, girl."

"T, pleeeeeeeeeeeeeease," I beg, sounding like a two-year-old pleading for a cookie. Suddenly, I remember offering Noel my cookie. *Make it go away!* I silently pray to whatever god hates me so much as to let me make such an ass out of myself.

"Nope. The King is hot for you, and you need to face the music."

"Hand me my phone," I tell her, not bothering to use my manners and say please. What kind of best friend would bail at a time like this?

Once I turn my phone on, I see that I already have a text from Byron.

FitzAssoc: How are you feeling?

AiméeT: What did he do, take out an ad and tell everyone?!

FitzAssoc: Not that I know of. The state of his office was a little surprising this morning, so I asked. I hear you had yourself a little dinner date.

AiméeT: Oh, Byron, I blew it BIG time!

FitzAssoc: Fun!!!

AiméeT: Not that, you pig. Get your mind out of the gutter!

FitzAssoc: Pardon me, your ladyship. I didn't mean to offend.

AiméeT: Noel bought me the best meal I've ever eaten. Then I got drunk on some fancy Beaujolais, and then ... I made it clear what I wanted for dessert. -face of shame-

FitzAssoc: And? Was he any good? Because I have to tell you, I've thought about it extensively and I'm reasonably sure the man has some skills.

AiméeT: That's the worst part. He turned me down.

FitzAssoc: Ah, the burden of a gentleman. You know they're raised not to take advantage of ladies in a certain way.

AiméeT: Drunk women?

FitzAssoc: That would be the way.

AiméeT: I can never see him again, Byron. Never ever ever. Ever.

FitzAssoc: I don't understand your reasoning. Clearly, he wanted to go for it but thought too highly of you to take advantage.

AiméeT: I couldn't face him. What would I say?

FitzAssoc: How about, "Thank you for the nice meal?" or "Now that I'm sober, what do you say?"

AiméeT: Byron! Be serious!!

FitzAssoc: I am one hundred percent serious. If you propositioned my boss sober, he'd take you up on that faster than you can say, "Long live the queen!"

I stop texting long enough to imagine him taking me up on *that* and Whew! I like what I see.

AiméeT: Can you get the information about where he left my van for me?

FitzAssoc: I could try, but what fun would that be?

AiméeT: Byron, please.

FitzAssoc: Fine. But you should know that when I got in to work this morning, there was a memo on my desk about you starting our employee appreciation lunch this Friday. The boss also said I'm to give you an advance of five hundred dollars for supplies, so you'll have to pop up here to get your check.

Five hundred dollars?! I won't be out of pocket for once. I do a little seated happy dance, then realize I really do have to go up there, which means I very well may see him. And worse, *he* may see *me*.

AiméeT: Any chance he'll be out of the office today?

And every Friday forever?

FitzAssoc: Not that I know of. Now, I really need to go do my job. The boss is watching me and I'm pretty sure he's on to the fact that I haven't started the filing he left on my desk an hour ago.

AiméeT: Sounds awful. If I text you right before I come up, can you run to the elevator and hand me the check so I don't have to get off?

FitzAssoc: Coward.

AiméeT: And proud of it. Will you?

FitzAssoc: As you wish.

AiméeT: Princess Bride reference?

FtizAssoc: Of course.

AiméeT: Why are you not straight? Seriously?

FitzAssoc: Life's an ironic bitch sometimes. Now I really must get back to work.

AiméeT: xoxo

I put my phone down, feeling like I've just signed my own death warrant. First thing's first though. I need to brush my teeth about six times to remove the fuzzy socks they're wearing—a predictable result of my wild ways—and then I need a scalding hot shower.

Only then will I pick up my van.

Chapter Eighteen

Noel

I really have gone too far this time. Trying to convince her to proposition me again? That crossed the line. And talking up my sexual prowess? Pathetic. She can never find out it's me. Never. I really do have to tell Byron, especially if she's going to be here every week. I can't risk her figuring out that she's not texting him. If that happens, she'll despise me forever, which is a possibility I can't stomach. What a shite situation. I don't want her to love me, but I can't live in a world where she hates me either, as selfish as that sounds.

I've manipulated her. Treated her like all those other men. Lying to get what I want from her. This is the *only* time I've ever done something even remotely like this. I've always played it straight with the other women I've dated. It's not my fault they didn't believe the truth about my priorities. They all thought that at some point they'd end up at the top of the list.

What they didn't understand was that I had the financial security of dozens of families resting firmly on my shoulders. It's a burden I take with the utmost gravity. When you hire people, they make a promise to work hard for you, and you make a promise right back—that you're going to make sure they'll have a job to come to every day. And since I started my own firm nine years ago, I've lived up to that promise. I would never jeopardize the well-being of my employees for any reason, including my own happiness.

When I was younger and naïve, I thought I could juggle my responsibilities with a relationship, but I learned the hard way it couldn't be done. And until now, I've stuck to my guns, allowing no one to get in the way of my goals.

But this time?

This time, I've broken all my own rules, and in a most despicable way. I've let myself down, but worse, I've lied to Aimée over and over again. I sigh, walking over to the window, wondering if she's on her way here yet and what I should do when she arrives. Maybe I should just tell Byron she's in a big rush and ask him to meet her at the elevator with the money. But knowing him, he'll hop on with her and ride down so he can dig up some dirt about last night. He really was rather shocked by the state of my office when he came in this morning.

I turn and look at him through the glass wall. At least I didn't lie about him not doing the filing. He's been talking up the FedEx guy for the last twenty minutes. If he were anyone other than my twin, he'd have been fired so long ago. His phone rings and he gives the guy the "one sec" finger before answering. He turns and gestures to me urgently, mouthing, "Walter Junior!" I hurry to my desk just as my phone rings and pick it up. "Noel Fitzwilliam."

"Noel, it's Walter, the younger, better version."

Doing my best to sound casual, I say, "Walter, how are you?"

"Never better. Listen, I got your message about meeting for lunch. I have to say I feel like the prettiest girl at the prom. You architects are a hungry bunch."

I ball up my free fist, then do my best to let the offending comment slide off my back. I let out a friendly chuckle that makes me hate myself. "Well, it's a hell of an amazing opportunity you boys are offering. You can't blame us for wanting in on it, right?"

"Makes me glad I'm me and not you," he says with an almost girly giggle that causes me to want to reach through the phone with two fingers and poke him in the eyes.

"Right. Sure," I say. "So, I'm assuming you gave some thought to our proposal. As I said in the meeting, it's our starting point, but we want to work with your team to give you exactly what you're looking for. In the end, you have a vision for this city, and we're here to help you make that a reality."

"Yeah, I remember your spiel," Walter answers. "Actually, it's almost word-for-word what the other guys said." There's that giggle again. Grrr…

"Any architect worth his salt knows it's all about pleasing the client," I say, doing my best not to sound defensive. Or insulted. Or annoyed.

"I'm pretty sure all the ladies of the night have that same motto." He snort-laughs, then says, "Sorry, man. I don't mean to offend. I'm just playing with you."

"Right," I grind out. "No problem."

"Glad you've got a sense of humor. I don't work with people who can't take a joke. I'll let you in on a little secret. We're leaning toward you, but we're pretty much going to need a complete overhaul of your design by the end of next month if we're going to sign off on it."

I shut my eyes tightly, not wanting to let that sink in. A complete overhaul *before* they sign. That's pretty much worst-case scenario. Well, other than a no right out of the gate.

He continues with, "Anyway, I know you're anxious to get some face-time with me, and my squash game just fell through. Do you play?"

No, I do not play squash. "Only a couple of times in uni."

"Excellent, that means I can squash you like a bug." *Egad, this man is annoying.* "Meet me at the Albany Club on 53rd at one p.m. We can work up a sweat and talk deets."

He hangs up before I have a chance to say no. Not that I would. Sitting back in my chair, I let out a long, frustrated sigh. I guess I have to go buy some trainers and shorts. Oh, and a racquet. But first I need to figure out what to do about Aimée.

Chapter Nineteen

Aimée

I spend so much time getting ready to go downtown and pick up my van you'd think I was preparing for the Miss America pageant. There's showering, exfoliating, double leg shaving, moisturizing, hair drying, hair curling, and makeup— all before trying to figure out what to wear. Cute spring dress with a fluttery hem.

On the off chance that I actual see Noel, I need to make sure I look and smell so good that he kicks himself all over hell and back for turning me down last night. Meanwhile, I'll act all light and happy and totally oblivious that anything is up. That'll show him who's boss. Me, I'm the boss.

By the time I'm walking into the lobby, I've actually talked myself into wanting to see him. Or rather, I've decided he *needs* to see me. When the elevator opens, I step out and spot Byron. I'm about to run over to him and throw myself into his arms and thank him for being such a great friend, but Noel walks out of his office and blocks me.

He mutters something to Byron, who, in turn, walks in the opposite direction. Drat. I remind myself to smile. Smile like someone's giving me a thousand bucks for every visible tooth.

When Noel reaches me, he furrows his brow and asks, "How are you feeling?"

"Never better!" I practically shout at him. "Seriously, really good! Thank you so much for breakfast!" *OMG, stop yelling at him, already.*

"I always find a full-English does the trick after a night of too much fun." He winks at me and my insides spasm like I've just shuffled through shag carpeting while wearing wool socks before grabbing the refrigerator handle. What are the chances Byron is right and I can talk Noel into making up for last night's lack of physical intimacy just by showing up here sober?

"Would you mind if I used your bathroom before I go get my van?" My plan is to invade his inner sanctum then BAM! pounce like a panther.

Noel walks me in the opposite direction of his office and says, "There's a ladies' room right here."

Oh. I give him a semi-smile—four and a half front teeth showing tops, no bottoms, and definitely no molars. I don't really have to go to the bathroom, but I can't tell him that, so I turn around and walk in.

Oh hurray, Cindy's standing at the sink, washing her claws. "Hi, Cindy," I say, feeling the need to say something. The woman did let me wear her pants, after all.

She eyes me in the mirror like I'm a cockroach in her soup. "I'm sorry, do I know you?"

Ah, so we're going to play this game, are we? "Aimée Tompkins," I tell her. "The caterer from last Friday's lunch. You lent me your pants."

"Right." She sounds SO enthused. "I'm actually surprised they fit you," she says while looking me up and down, still in the mirror.

Not even having the courtesy to turn and look at me in person is really ticking me off. So much so, I say, "They were actually big. I had to wear two aprons so that people wouldn't see how they hung on me." I'm filing this little scene away for further enjoyment.

Cindy rears back like I slapped her, but I ignore her and go wait in a stall until she leaves. Don't mess with me, Cindy of the torturous pants. I will slay you!

After I hear the door close—Slam! I come out, reapply my lipstick, and fluff my hair in the mirror. I look good. You know how after a night of too much alcohol your face can puff up a little? I've decided it's a flattering look on me. It probably takes off a couple years. Add the bee-stung lips, I gotta confess, I'm hard-pressed not to lean into the mirror and kiss myself.

Noel is waiting for me when I come out. "If you're ready, I can take you to the garage to get your van," he says.

"You're going to go with me? What a gentleman!" I'm yelling again.

He leads me to the elevator while I turn around looking for Byron. I see him walk back to his desk and when our eyes connect, I wink at him and give him a big thumbs up. He smiles distractedly like he doesn't even know me. Oh, I get it, we're going to be professional in front of other people. That makes sense.

Noel holds the elevator door for me before getting on himself. He stands so close I can smell the spices in his aftershave. Yummmmmmmmmm. People get on and off, so I don't even try to carry on a conversation with him, I just lean in and inhale his essence. When we're nearing the eighth floor, he looks down at me and we just stare at each other. I smile and bat my eyelashes, but he doesn't return my flirty gaze. There's a tiny vertical line between his eyebrows that makes me wonder if he's worried about something.

When we get off at the lobby, Noel says, "Should we walk? It's a lovely day and I wouldn't mind stretching my legs, if you're up for it."

Oh, I'm up for it all right. "Sounds great. I love walking. And being outside. And walking outside," I ramble on while he holds open the door for me. "I really appreciate you coming with me, but I know how busy you are so if you don't have time …" *Come anyway because I think I'm falling in love with you and I really want you to ask me out again or kiss me or both.*

"I'm happy to take you," he says as we fall into step with each other on the wide sidewalk.

The sun shines down, warming my skin and making me feel more alive than I have in a very long time. Maybe ever. "This is my favorite time in the city—it's pretty and fresh and everything feels new. I bet London is nice in the spring too."

"I'm afraid it's rather rainy and dull," he answers as he sidesteps a man waiting in line at a hot dog cart.

"Oh, well, it's better that you moved here then," I answer, wondering if it's too soon to ask if he plans on staying. Definitely too soon. We haven't even kissed yet.

"Aimée, there's something I want to discuss with you."

If I didn't have the pelvic floor that I do, I might have peed myself. He's going to tell me that he wants to take me on a real date *and* all that might entail. I can barely contain my excitement.

"The thing is," he says, sounding way too serious for the good news he's about to impart. "I like you very much."

"I like you very much too," I tell him, wondering why he doesn't sound more enthusiastic.

"Yes, well, in my case, the number of people I like could fit on a Post-It note. Actually, one of those Post-It tabs used to indicate where to sign a document."

I grin at a woman pushing a stroller as I walk past, imagining myself saying, *He likes me, and he doesn't like anyone else. Also, where'd you get that stroller, because I may need one in a couple years.* "So I've been admitted into a pretty exclusive club, then."

"Very," he says with a sigh. "You are warm and bright and smart and really, really fun. And I find myself thinking about you a lot more than I probably should."

"That's okay. Think away," I answer, wondering if he's finally about to stop walking, spin me to him and plant one on me right here on Wall Street.

"But ..." No buts! Nononononononono!!! I somehow manage not to yell that, but it's a close one. "It wouldn't be fair to you if I were to try to turn this into ... more. I'm not in a position to get involved with anyone right now."

I'm not going to lie. That hurt like a bee sting to the eyeball. "Oh, right, okay. I mean sure, I totally understand. I'm your caterer." I blink so quickly, I'm not watching where I'm going anymore. This results in me tripping on a corner of broken concrete, lunging forward before catching myself, falling forward again, and finally plunging to my knees where I use a metal garbage can to catch my face. By my teeth.

Oh god, the PAIN! The pain is so, so bad. My mouth fills with blood and when Noel hauls me onto my feet and turns me to him, he gasps. "Oh, my god! Your poor mouth."

"Is it bad?" I lisp, spitting blood all over my pretty sundress (and Noel's shirt).

He winces and nods. "Your front tooth is ... well it's missing the bottom half."

I reach up and touch my teeth, only to realize that the right one is now extremely short and jagged. And I have no money to get it fixed so I'm going to end up looking like some sort of hillbilly. Aimée, the hillbilly caterer from Rochester. I should remake my business cards.

The man of my dreams is staring at me, likely shocked and disgusted by the very sight. It's the perfect cherry on the sundae after being told he's not that into me. The pain of all of it together knocks my last thread of composure loose and I burst into tears.

For the record, I'm not a delicate crier. No, sir. I go straight from watering eyes to great heaving sobs. As soon as I feel the snot run down my nose, I come completely unglued.

The look on Noel's face is one of amazement with a healthy dose of underlying horror. Clearly, he's not used to highly emotional women. "Oh, Aimée," he croons pulling me into his arms. "I'm so sorry. Are you okay?"

I don't know whether he's referencing the missing tooth, the blood dripping down my knees, or my broken heart. But I don't have the strength to convincingly lie to him. Yet, I still try. "Yup!" I squeak as I pull away. "Totally fine. You shouldn't feel sorry for me. I mean, I get it. I threw myself at you and you weren't interested. It's fine. I'm your caterer and that's all I'll ever be and that's okay. Fine, actually. Being your caterer is good. I need money more than I need a boyfriend." I wonder if he'll pick up on how many times I'm reminding him I'm his caterer. I really do need the money.

I dare to glance up at him and he looks alarmed by my display. I sniff the snot back into my head and dig into my purse to pull out some old tissues, hoping they're not used. I slap two directly onto my bloody knees and let them hang there in hopes of stopping the flow of blood, then I hold a bunch up to my mouth. I must look so, so bad right now. But what does it matter?

Noel is not interested in me. Big sigh followed by a hiccup or two.

"Aimée," Noel says again. "We should get you to a dentist immediately."

"No, not we. You have to work. I'll take myself."

"Are you sure? What if they have to give you laughing gas or something? You'll need someone to get you home."

"Well, it certainly won't be you. That would be something a boyfriend would do. Not someone you work for on a casual basis every Friday indefinitely," I say, my words muffled by the tissue. "Besides you're too busy. And I'm not being passive-aggressive. You really are."

He rubs the back of his neck. "I do have a rather pressing meeting, but maybe I could rearrange my schedule or get Byron to go with you?"

"I'm fine, seriously. Just show me to my van."

Noel pauses for a second before saying, "If that's what you want."

I don't answer him. I've done enough talking. I've made a total fool out of myself and I'm not looking to do it again any time soon. If he has something to say to me, he can say it, otherwise we can walk in silence.

After a few minutes, he finally speaks up. "I work all the time. It wouldn't be fair to you or me to get involved right now."

"Sure, fine, I get it."

"What do you get?" he pushes.

"I get that you're a busy and important man and that you don't have time for me."

He takes my hand in his. "Not having time to date has nothing to do with being important. I really don't have time."

I want to ask him what last night was all about if he doesn't have time for romance. It very much looked like we were on a date, and if I hadn't gotten shit-faced, that date might have ended on a very high note. But, you know, whatever.

When we get to the parking garage, Noel opens his wallet and pulls out three twenties to pay the attendant. *He parked my van in a garage that charges sixty dollars a night? Is he insane?* "I don't have that kind of cash on me right now, but I'll pay you back," I tell him.

"Nonsense. This is on me."

I unlock the door and get in the passenger side before asking, "Can I at least give you a lift back to the office?"

He shakes his head slowly. "No, thanks, I think I'll walk." He won't even drive ten blocks with me. Wow, when he's done with a woman, he's really done. Or maybe it's because I look like a character from Bugs Bunny who just got smacked in the face with an anvil. Or it could be because I totally turned him off last night by throwing myself at him.

Or—and this is the worst thought—he never wanted me in the first place.

Tears free-fall down my face, but I don't say anything. I just close my door, buckle-up, and drive away without looking back.

Chapter Twenty

Noel

"Oof!" I grunt as my body slams against the white wall of the squash court.

Walter makes a "whoop!" sound, then asks, "You're not just letting me win so you get the contract, are you?"

"No," I answer, which is sadly true. "I'm just a bit rusty."

"A bit! Does that mean the opposite in England?" He swipes at the floor, retrieving the dark blue ball. Why, that son of a bitch, I want to wipe the floor with his face. He drops the ball and smacks it with a smirk that says he knows I'm about to lunge like a fool and miss yet again. Which I do.

We've been playing for close to an hour now, and I've drenched my new shorts and T-shirt with sweat. I'm so soaked that my stupid goggle things keep sliding down my nose, distracting me and forcing me to stab at them with my finger during the rallies. Well, if there were rallies. It's pretty much just him serving five times in a row and racking up points, then me serving five that he easily hits back, thus ending the play.

To be honest, I can't concentrate for more than thirty seconds at a time. I cannot stop thinking about Aimée and her knees and her mouth and the hurt in her eyes. I want to climb out of the oddly tiny door, find out where she is, and rush to her side. But I can't very well do that, can I? Not after I've gone and rejected her.

"Game point," Walter says. "If I get this one, it'll be ten games to zero."

"Brilliant," I mutter.

And here comes the ball.

And there goes the ball … and my stupid paddle or whatever it's called. Honestly, I'm so tired, I don't even care to pick it up. I'll just leave the bloody thing here.

I bend at the waist and rest my hands on my knees while Walter grabs my racquet for me and hands it to me. "What do you say to a beer?"

"Yes. I'm much better at holding a pint than a racquet."

Fifteen minutes later, we've both showered and changed and are seated in the small bar area of the club. Walter holds up two fingers and a middle-aged waitress with big hair gives him a nod.

"You lasted longer than I thought you would," he says, grabbing a handful of salted peanuts from the communal bowl (which I would never touch—this place is probably crawling with single-shake guys).

"Well, I try to workout. I do some running and weights here and there."

"No, I meant, you lasted a long time without asking about the project."

"Oh, that. Well, I like to do one thing at a time as poorly as possible," I say with a grin.

The waitress drops two glasses of a light ale at our table. Walter looks up and says, "Thanks, Honey."

I start to feel offended on her behalf before I check her name tag. Huh, her name actually is Honey.

"No problem, Walt," she says with a wink. "Who's your friend?"

"This is Noel. He's from England."

"Well, hello Noel from England. Fancy seeing someone from your neck of the woods on this side of the pond."

"Yes, well, I live here now," I answer politely.

"Ooh, that accent is what my friends and I call the panty-melter."

I choke on what was supposed to be my first sip of beer, then manage to say, "Thank you?" But it comes out as a question.

"You let me know if you need anything else," she says with a wink. "I'll take real good care of you."

The bartender calls her name, and she hurries off to pick up another order, leaving Walter and me to deal with the matter at hand. I decide the direct approach is the best. "So, you said you're going to need to see a lot of changes to the design. Does that mean you'd like to go ahead with us?"

He tilts his head and screws up his face in a "not sure" sort of way. "Listen, if it were up to me, we'd be going with you. But my dad is really pushing hard for Lassiter and Sons, and since he's not going to retire until this building is standing, I can't exactly overrule him. Not yet, anyway."

"Pity, I figured you for the man in charge."

He puffs up a little and says, "I am for the day-to-day stuff. And I'm the guy the staff comes to for decisions, but this one is different. Dad sees it as his swan song." Taking a swig of his beer, he says, "Can't blame him though. The old man's been in the business for thirty-eight years. It's natural that he'd want to make his mark before he disappears to Florida to spend his days lawn bowling."

"Makes sense," I say. "You're a good son to respect him enough to listen to him, especially when he's on his way out."

"I have to. If I don't play this right, he might decide to stay."

"Ah," I say with a nod. "So, Walter, what do I need to do to help you get what you want?"

The smile on his face makes me more than a little nervous. He raises his hand to Honey, and when she comes back, he asks to be brought a whole bottle of tequila.

Chapter Twenty-One

Aimée

I drive my van straight to Bean Town. Not because I want to go into work looking like I was just hit in the face by a wrecking ball, but because I need to see my best friend. I need some compassion and a shoulder to cry on, stat. Also, Kwan might have another cousin who's a dentist who could fix my tooth in his living room, or back alley. I'm not particular.

I park illegally in the loading zone out front before turning on my emergency lights. Hopefully that'll keep the meter maid from ticketing me. Then I hobble into the bakery.

Teisha is foaming milk for a cappuccino when she looks up and sees me. "Holy sweet mother of Jesus on the cross! What happened to you?" She drops the metal container holding the milk and rushes toward me. "Do you need an ambulance?"

Her concern opens the flood gates once again. The tears and snot cue my bloody lip to start gushing again. "Call 911!" T yells to the concerned crowd that's starting to form.

"No … no … no …" I hiccup. "I just fell and cracked my tooth. I don't neeeeeeeeeeeeeeed an ambulance." It's like my emotional bubble got so full that it popped, and is spewing its contents everywhere. Every. Where.

There are no free tables so T walks up to two businessmen and says, "Time to leave, fellas. Scoot." When they don't move fast enough, she yells, "NOW!" As they beat it out of Dodge, she ushers me to an empty chair and soothes, "I'll get some tea and cookies." She stares at my tooth. "Maybe rice pudding. Will you be okay for a minute?"

Nodding my head, I start the process of trying to pull myself together. A sketchy looking twenty-something man approaches me with a smile on his face. *Dude, you're not going to try to hit on me now, are you? Not the time.*

He opens his wallet and hands me a slip of paper. "I'm a dental student," he tells me. "I can set you up with a cap on that tooth for a fraction of the price a real dentist would charge. Call me." Then he walks away.

First of all, ew. Who tries to drum up business like that? And also, maybe, if Kwan doesn't have a lead for me.

Teisha comes back and places a cup of tea and two scones in front of me. Then she hands me a plastic baggie full of ice. "We're out of pudding. Now, what happened, hon?" she demands as she plops down in the seat across from me.

"Oh, T, it was so bad, so very bad." I explain all about how I thought Noel was about to ask me out for real, but instead of doing that, he squashed my heart like a bug under his shoe. "Then I tripped and fell into a garbage can. Then I ... I ... I ..." I stop for a moment to blubber.

Another man walks over and hands me his business card. What the ...? I don't even look at him before yelling, "I am not going to a dental school to have my tooth fixed!"

"I'm a lawyer," he says. "Looks like you might have cause for a lawsuit."

"Who am I going to sue?" I demand.

"The owner of that garbage can."

"Are you serious? You think I should sue someone for having their garbage can exactly where it belongs?" What's he smoking?

"You could sue the city for that crack on the sidewalk." Does he have our table bugged? How did he hear me say that?

Teisha rolls her eyes and interjects, "Why don't you sue the company that made her shoes that caused her to trip?"

"That's a great idea ..." he starts to say.

He doesn't finish that thought because T interrupts by shouting, "Get out of here, you bottom feeder!"

He shrugs his shoulders and walks away like this is normal treatment. Which for him, it probably is.

My friend refocuses her attention on me. "So, no you and Noel, huh?"

I shrug my shoulders.

"But you got the catering gig, right?"

"I hope. I mean, I think I did. Although he might be reconsidering my employment after the scene I subjected him to." *Two years of White Gloves and Party Manner lessons as a child down the drain.*

"Don't worry about that. Just text Byron and let him take care of it."

"But then I'll have to see Noel every week," I complain.

"No, you won't. I'll cover for you if you want. We can even hire Jennifer the dog walker to help out if we need to."

I nod my head pathetically. That's not a bad idea. I'll need to hire a lot of people if I actually get this business up and running, which I'm determined to do, especially now that I've decided to give up on dating. Forever.

"I'm gonna go home," I tell T. "Can you ask Kwan if he knows a place where I can get my tooth fixed for cheap?"

She nods her head. "You betcha. In the meantime, go get some rest and I'll see you at home in a couple of hours."

I wrap my scones in a paper napkin and head out to my van. Luckily, I find parking just down the block from T's apartment, so I'll have a few hours before I have to move it uptown to my space in the Bronx.

Once I'm curled up on the couch under a cozy throw, I pick up my phone and text Byron.

AiméeT: Oh, Byron. Today went so wrong. I thought Noel was going to tell me how much he liked me and how he couldn't wait to go out on a date with me, but that isn't what happened at all.

I wait for him to text back. When he doesn't, I continue:

AiméeT: He said he liked me, but he didn't have time for me. I think that's code for "You're not classy enough for me." What do you think?

No answer, so I keep going.

AiméeT: I thought I was taking the rejection pretty well until I tripped on the sidewalk and did a header into a garbage can. I landed on my face, so my lip is the size of my head. I chipped a tooth, and my knees look like raw hamburger. I'm embarrassed, heartbroken, and look like the world's worst boxer.

Nothing.

AiméeT: Where are you?!!!

AiméeT: Fine, don't be there for me in my hour of need. But I tell you this. If Walter Junior still wants to go out with me after seeing my sad new face, I might just let him jump the line on my fifth date rule. It's not like I need a man to make me feel better about myself, but I could sure use the comfort of a strong pair of arms around me right now.

When Byron doesn't text back, I close my eyes and try to let my brain take a break from my real life. Unfortunately, it's not on board with that idea and all it wants to do is think about Noel.

Chapter Twenty-Two

Noel

I am drunk. It's taken me a ridiculously long time to unlock the door to my apartment, which normally isn't a problem for me. Yay, me. I'm a man of many talents. I can use a key whilst sober. I kick the door shut behind me and dump my squash bag (that will never be used again) on the entryway console.

It's only just after six, but I already want to climb under the covers—with one foot on the floor to stop the room from spinning—and pretend this day is over. I've gone from ordering breakfast for the woman I fancy to dumping her so I don't hurt her (only to hurt her). From there I moved on to being creamed at a stupid racquet game by Walter the Wanker Junior, who then forced me to drink shot for shot—ostensibly to prove my manhood after that arse-beating he gave to me— while he spills all the secrets about what will cause daddy dearest to sign on the dotted line.

After his first few shots, he started talking and I started listening with both ears. Thankfully, I managed to pour half of my drinks into a large planter behind me but even so, I'm pissed. Walter has got to be an alcoholic to put away so much booze without being in a coma right now.

It sounds like Lassiter and Sons has been playing some dirty pool that got Junior and Senior into a big fight over where their loyalties lie. Thank God we didn't accept that sneak peek at their presentation. It would have come back to bite a huge chunk out of my arse.

The entire ride home I jotted down notes—everything I could remember in my inebriated state. I only hope I'll be able to read my chicken scratch in the morning. The bottom line is that if we're going to have a shot at One Rosenthal, we need to have a brand-new design ready in fewer than six weeks. Basically, they want the back to be the front and the top to be the bottom. They love the eco-friendly elements, but they want an invisible rainwater system (no problem, right? I'll just hire the folks who made Wonder Woman's jet to build it). In addition, they want a forty-foot living wall in the lobby which means removing a load-bearing wall on the second, third, and fourth floors, which also means a whole lot of other changes and calculations. Since it took our team eight months to do the first one, I can't really see anyway in hell that we'll be able to pull it off.

But that's future Noel's problem. Current Noel is going to drink a gallon of water and take four aspirin so he won't want to walk off his tenth-floor balcony when he wakes up.

I kick off my dress shoes and pad toward my ultra-modern kitchen. Once there, I open the fridge. My phone buzzes in my pocket and my insides tighten. It's probably poor Aimée, trying to get a hold of her confidant, Byron, for advice. I sigh and force myself to look. I haven't written her back because I feel like an absolute cad. I'm the last person who should know how upset she is. She clearly wants me to think the entire thing is no biggie, but now she's considering revenge sex with Walter Junior?

That's a terrible idea for several reasons, the first of which being that she's mad at me, so by rights, if she wants to take her anger out on someone, she should really take it out on me. Honestly, the thought of her in anyone else's arms gives me heartburn that I feel across my entire body, so bodyburn, I guess? I don't know, I'm drunk.

Also, Walter Junior is a real knob, which I discovered by spending the whole bloody day with him. That whole "nice guy" act he put on for Aimée yesterday was just that—an act. Third, he's one of those obnoxious "walks around fully nude in the dressing room" guys, and honestly, there isn't much to see.

My phone buzzes again and I grab it and swipe the screen.

SexyCaterer: Byron, where are you? Text me as soon as you get this. I need the male perspective. Plus, you know your jackass of a boss better than I do, and maybe you can make sense out of this for me. Or you know, talk him into liking me again … -sad face-

WHITNEY DINEEN & MELANIE SUMMERS

Oh, god. This is awful. Just awful. I've never been privy to the behind-the-scenes carnage of a break-up before, but this is absolutely gut-wrenching. The crazy bit is we weren't really even dating. It was only the *potential* of dating. I am not only drunk. I'm an arsehole.

> Me: Hey you. Sorry I've been MIA. The boss has had me running all afternoon. Just got home. He said you hurt your face?! Are you okay?
>
> SexyCaterer: There you are. Thank God. It's so bad.

She attaches a photo of her with her enormously swollen lips spread, and a gap where her front right tooth should be. It makes my knees go weak and I slide onto a stool at the island.

> Me: Is that just now? Didn't you go to a dentist??
>
> SexyCaterer: Not yet. I have a friend of a friend trying to find someone I can afford, but the chances are slim, and he may be an amateur. To get the real deal to fix it, it'd probably be a couple thousand. IDK, I may have to wait a few months and save up. Until then, I'm going to have to talk with one hand over my mouth. Or mumble a lot. Or go to the Party Store and get vampire teeth. It could be my thing, you know, like how the queen wears bright colors?

Bloody hell, I cannot leave her like this. It's my fault she got hurt in the first place. If I hadn't upset her, she would've been looking where she was going and she wouldn't have tripped. But it's not like I can offer to pay. She's too proud to accept my help.

Me: I'll call in a favor. My dentist owes me one. I got him some great tickets to the Knicks once.

SexyCaterer: No, I can't let you use your favor up on me.

Me: Have you seen my teeth? I'm never going to need to call it in. Besides, you can pay me in extra treats when you come to the office every week.

SexyCaterer: Are you sure? Also, does this mean Noel doesn't want to fire me?

Me: I'm sure and he definitely doesn't. He's not the kind to kick a person when they're down.

SexyCaterer: Too bad he's the kind to lead a girl on, get her hopes up, then crush her like a peanut shell.

Ouch. I am such an arse.

Me: Oh, Aimée, forget about him. He's not worth your time. He's a workaholic, which is only slightly better (maybe) than dating a crackhead or a guy who frequents Comic Con.

SexyCaterer: Or a sadist.

Me: More like a masochist, if he let you go.

SexyCaterer: Aww, you're so sweet.

I pause to down a good half-gallon of water in hopes of being a functioning human being by tomorrow.

Me: When I was a kid, I took a knock to the side of the head from a chap at school that made me dizzy for a month. The problem was, I was afraid of him after that. And adolescent boys can smell fear like it's a chocolate cake.

SexyCaterer: While I appreciate your telling me this, what's your point?

Me: I don't want you wearing your heart on your sleeve with my boss. He's a good guy, but you need to be strong. Hold your head up high and forget him.

I'm telling her this not only so she never feels like I'm worth her sadness, but because I can't be strong if I witness it, and she deserves so much better than I can offer her.

SexyCaterer: Okay, T just got home. We're going to watch He's Just Not That Into You so I can feel like I'm not the only loser on the planet.

Me: You are not a loser. You deserve better than Noel. You really do.

SexyCaterer: Do NOT tell me "he's" out there somewhere and you promise to help me find him because we both know that's BS.

Me: Okay, I won't.

Mostly because I can't stomach the thought of her finding someone else.

I do a quick Google search of highly rated dentists in Manhattan and jot down the numbers of the top four. I'll call first thing in the morning and go with whoever can fit her in fastest. Then I wander over to the sofa and surf through the shows on Netflix. I settle on *He's Just Not That Into You.* This day has been such a total cock up, the least I can do is watch the same thing as the woman I think I love. *Please tell me that's the tequila talking.*

Chapter Twenty-Three

Aimée

My entire body aches like I've fallen out of a plane and lived to tell the tale. I roll over on my mattress on T's floor and groan for all I'm worth. "Owie!" I whimper as I try to sit up. Then I call out, "T!" No answer. So, I call louder, "Teishaaaaaaaaaaaaaaaaa!!!" Nothing. So much for my getting a handful of aspirin delivered to my bedside.

When I get to the kitchen counter, I find a note saying that T went out to get donuts for us. I'm starting to feel a little guilty about all she's doing for me. Thank goodness I've nursed her through her share of heartaches, or this relationship would definitely be feeling lopsided.

Too bad neither of us is into girls or we could just settle into domestic bliss and forget men even exist. Alas, we don't play for that team, men exist, and our need for fried fatty dough knows no bounds.

I pick up my phone and check my texts.

FitzAssoc: You have an eleven a.m. appoint with Dr. Pearlman on Fifth Avenue. Text me back and let me know if you can make it.

I look at the clock and see that it's already ten. Crap, I'm gonna have to book it if I'm going to make it downtown on time. I hurry to text Byron back.

AiméeT: You are a god among men! I hate reaping the benefits of your favor though. The only reason I'm taking you up on it is because I look like I should be sucking on a corncob pipe or spitting chewing tobacco through the gap. I'm scary. I promise to pay you back though, once I get a few of your employee appreciation lunches under my belt.

FitzAssoc: I won't hear of it! This is my gift to you, and it comes with heartfelt apologies that my boss is such a bloody wanker.

AiméeT: Well, when you put it like that. Lol. Also, Dr. Pearlman? What are the chances he made that up to suit his chosen profession?

FitzAssoc: He's legit. Of course, if you find out his first name is Bicuspid, then you might be on to something.

AiméeT: Stop! My face hurts too much to laugh. I'll text you when I'm done. I adore you!

FitzAssoc: I love you! Truly.

Tossing my phone into my purse so I don't forget it, I feel a glow of happiness that makes me want to throw handfuls of candy to the masses like

I'm a May Queen riding on a toilet paper float in a parade. Byron loves me. I think mama just scored herself a gay best friend which is a gift as special as a best girlfriend, but with the added benefits of insights into the male brain— such as it is.

I take a cab downtown until the traffic backs up around W 60th Street. That's when I pay the cabbie and run across the park for my appointment. I arrive sweaty and out of breath with a crazy "fleeing from an ax murderer" vibe. I'm no runner.

While looking around the office, I try to slow my breathing enough so I can actually talk. Wow, this place is probably way nicer than anything Kwan could've hooked me up with. Sleek leather furnishings and—wait for it—current magazines, like from this year. Dr. P must be rolling in it. The last time I went to a doctor's office there was a *People* magazine with a picture of Prince on the cover partying like it was 1999.

I don't have long to wait until I'm called back into Dr. Herschel B. Pearlman's office. The B does not stand for bicuspid. I asked and didn't receive as much as a titter of appreciation.

Dr. Pearlman appears to be a man with little sense of humor, which is a drag because funny is where I go when I'm nervous. And right now, sitting back in this dentist chair, staring at a fifty-something-year-old man's hair plugs, I'm scared out of my mind. *I hate going to the dentist.*

The dental technician is trying to match the color of my veneer while giving me quite the eyeful down her obviously tailored-for-her scrubs. I'm willing to bet she's applying for the role of mistress to one Dr. Herschel B. Pearlman. That is if she doesn't already have it.

The doctor tells me that he's going to make a temporary crown for my tooth today. My permanent crown will come in within two weeks. As he's digging around my mouth and making me bite down on some goo that forms a mold of my teeth, he says, "No hard food, no chewy foods, and no sticky food until the temporary comes off." What I'm getting from this is that I'm not allowed to eat for two weeks. Good times.

When I make my next appointment, I find myself curious about how big of a favor Dr. P. owes Byron, so I ask the receptionist, "How much is this going to cost, anyway?"

She pulls out my chart and settles down with a calculator. Number after number is punched in until I'm starting to worry this might rival the national debt. After I'm sure her fingers are worn to the bone, she announces, "With this visit, the next visit, the temp, and the crown, the total is going to be three-thousand-seven-hundred and twenty-five dollars."

"Holy Toledo!" I blurt out. That's more money than I can comprehend spending at the dentist in my entire lifetime. At the very least I should be walking out of here with an eighteen-karat gold grill.

"Don't worry," she tells me. "Your bill is being taken care of."

"Yeah, well, thank you. I'll be back in two weeks." I stroll out into the sunshine and ponder what it must be like for people who don't have to blink at an expense like that. I can't go into Duane Reade to buy a new mascara without wondering what the heck they put into the stuff to make it cost so much. And we're talking Maybelline here, not Chanel.

I find a nice park bench to sit on and pull out my phone. I'm going to pretend I live in this neighborhood for a hot minute.

> AiméeT: Hey, Byron it's me. I have a gorgeous temporary crown that I'm not allowed to let food near, so I'm thinking I'll probably be able to fit into Cindy's pants once I get the permanent.
>
> FitzAssoc: Don't you dare starve yourself into a skeleton! You're a sexy woman with curves. No one wants a bone but a dog.
>
> AiméeT: I thought you gay guys were supposed to be super fashion and body conscious. I only tell you this, so you don't lose your gay card by having a fat friend. Also, can I officially be your straight girlfriend now?
>
> FitzAssoc: Consider yourself promoted to fruit fly, darling.
>
> AiméeT: Why don't we get together and go out for drinks some time? It was super weird seeing you in the office yesterday and not jumping into your arms.
>
> FitzAssoc: We absolutely should!
>
> AiméeT: Where do live anyway?
>
> FitzAssoc: ...
>
> FitzAssoc: ...

AiméeT: Byron, you there?

FitzAssoc: Whoops, gotta go! The boss is due in any minute and he'll flip a biscuit if I don't have his coffee ready for him.

AiméeT: He's not in the office yet? I thought he lived there.

FitzAssoc: He had a late meeting last night. Where are you anyway? Are you still at the dentist's office?

AiméeT: I'm sitting on a park bench out front. I'm pretending I'm fancy enough to live in a neighborhood like this. Okay, I know you have to go. Text me later and let's set up a date.

FitzAssoc: ...

"Aimée, is that you?" I look up and stare into the luminous green eyes of one Noel Fitzwilliam.

"Noel? What are you doing here?"

"I live here," he tells me, while shoving his phone into his pocket.

"What do you mean you live here?" I look around like I've suddenly been transported to his living room or something.

He points to the building behind him. "I live there."

I shouldn't be surprised that Noel lives on Fifth Avenue with not one, but two liveried doormen. The disparity of our financial portfolios is truly staggering. He gets takeout from Daniel and lives in what I'm sure is a multi-million-dollar apartment, and I don't even buy a hot dog on the street because I can get a whole pack for the same price in the grocery store.

"I just got done at the dentist's office," I tell him, pointing my finger around the corner.

"You still look a bit swollen," he tells me. "Give us a smile and let me see."

I give him a half-hearted grin. "See? All better."

He suddenly sits down next to me. "Are you all better? Your lip looks ravaged."

"I'm right as rain." I jump up like I just hit the eject button on a fighter jet seat. "I better get going. I have to, um, get to work."

"Do you work somewhere other than catering?" He sounds surprised.

Nodding, I say, "Bean Town Bakery on Amsterdam Avenue."

"I've been there." He sounds surprised that we have something in common. "Best pumpkin muffin in the city."

"That's right." I shift uncomfortably from foot to foot. I want to throw myself into Noel's arms and beg him to love me. I want to tell him about all my great qualities and prove that I'm good enough for him. But he told me point blank yesterday that nothing could ever happen between us. He sounded very firm in his decision, so I merely offer another small smile.

"See ya," I tell him while I walk away. I pull out my phone and text Byron.

AiméeT: Your boss is a beautiful man. But just so you know, he totally broke my heart.

Chapter Twenty-Four

Noel

"Noel? Hello?" Cindy says, waving her hand in front of my face.

Bollocks. I'm doing it again. Daydreaming about a certain curvy caterer when I should be solidly focused on the massive undertaking at hand. "I'm sorry, you were saying ..."

"What is going on with you, Noel? You've been totally distracted today."

That's because I have this terrible feeling I've made a horrible mistake and will never be happy again. "I'm just tired. It's been a rather long week."

"Well, there's really no time to be tired because we have an ungodly deadline breathing down our neck. I'll tell Byron to get you a coffee," she says, picking up the conference room phone. "Yeah, Noel needs coffee. Actually, we could all use some. It's going to be another late night."

She's right. It will be. Another sixteen-hour day for me, followed by at least forty more until we have to present to the Walters again. Normally, I'd be completely energized by the challenge we're facing, but my creativity has taken a nose-dive. It's guilt. I know it. Aimée's text from yesterday pops into my mind: *Just so you know, he totally broke my heart,* as does my lame reply: *If he's not smart enough to scoop you up, you're better off.*

Byron appears in the doorway with a tray holding a carafe, several mugs, and the fixings. He sets it down on the side table and I thank him, before asking, "Can you order in some dinner for everyone?"

Byron nods. "Pizza or Chinese? Show of hands for za."

He does a quick count, then disappears, and leaves me alone with my exhausted staff. I glance around at their tired faces. "I know this has been a particularly trying time and I want you all to know I really am grateful. In fact, I was going to make it a surprise, but I've decided to hold a team appreciation lunch every Friday from now on, starting tomorrow."

Ali stares at me for a second. "That's really nice, but I'd rather be able to get home to my family earlier than sit at a two-hour lunch once a week. No offense."

"Do we even have time for that?" Jack asks.

"I, for one, think it's a great idea," Cindy says, batting her eyelashes at me.

No, Cindy, I'm not going to ask you to marry me. "I've hired a caterer to come in, actually."

"Not that Aimée person who bathes in perfume, I hope," Cindy sneers.

Sitting back in my chair, I raise one eyebrow. "Yes, actually. The lunch she served for our pitch was a real hit, but if you prefer, you can bring your own food."

Cindy shrugs, looking unimpressed. "No, that's fine. If you want to go that way, it's your call. Just tell her she can't borrow my pants again. I found weird little holes around the bottom hem. I don't know what she did to them."

"Ooh, is she going to make those cookies for us?" Jack asks. "I'm still dreaming about them."

I nod and smile to cover up the ridiculous pang in my chest at the thought of her cookies. *Seriously, Noel? Getting misty-eyed over baked goods now?*

I look back down at the schematics in front of me. "Okay, let's get back to it …"

Cindy picks up where I assume she left off a few minutes ago and I start daydreaming, even though I really should be listening. But I don't want to listen to boring Cindy drone on, even though she's talking about my favorite topic—design. Also, the thought of seeing Aimée tomorrow has me all tangled up and I suddenly regret telling her she could cater a lunch here every week. Seeing her that often after everything that's happened—and didn't happen—is going to be pure torture.

Of course, it's not like I can back out now. Not if I don't want to cross the line to complete wanker. Urgh, I need to tell Byron about that whole texting thing before she gets here in the morning. I know I should have told him before, but it's such a hard thing for me to admit—I'm the sensible, responsible rule-follower. He is NEVER going to let it go. Like N-E-V-E-R. We'll be sitting in a nursing home in side-by-side wheelchairs someday and he'll say, "Remember that time you pretended to be me so you could have phone sex with that caterer?" And I'll roll my eyes and say, "Yes." And he'll say, "That was the stupidest, most pathetic thing you ever did."

And he'll be right.

Yet, I still have to tell him, don't I? And it has to be done tonight.

We tie up our staff meeting at eleven. Seven of us, including me, opt to sleep on couches at the office so we can hit the ground with our feet running in the morning. Cindy sidles up to me and whispers, "Your pull-out couch is big enough for two. Do you mind sharing?"

"Not at all," I tell her before calling out to Byron. "You're sleeping with me tonight, Byron."

He turns around like I just ordered him to have a hot tar facial. "What a lovely offer, but I'm going home."

"I'm afraid that's not going to happen." I send him my sternest I'm-your-boss-and not-your-brother glare. I follow that up with a pleading I'll-buy-you-opening-night-tickets-to any-Broadway-musical-you-want-to see-for-an-entire-year look.

"Fine." He slams the stack of papers he's holding down on the conference table. "But if you hog the covers, we're through!"

Cindy leans in. "Byron is as big as you are. Surely that little mattress would work better for the two of us." This must be what it's like when Cruella De Vil is hitting on someone. I'm positively terrified.

"I'm good, Cindy, but thank you for being so concerned for my comfort." *Take the hint already.*

When she huffs off, I tell my brother, "We need to talk. My office, now."

"Unless you're calling me in there to give me a raise, I'm going straight to bed."

"Byron ..." I sound pathetic. "I've made a mess of things with Aimée and I need your help."

"Aimée who? There's no Aimée that works here." He looks confused. *Dear Lord, I do not look forward to this conversation.*

"Aimée the caterer," I tell him.

He rubs his hands together in gleeful enthusiasm. "Oh, this *is* going to be good. Should I pop some popcorn for the occasion?"

I roll my eyes at him. "Do whatever you want, just be in my office in two minutes." My brother walks down the hall so closely behind me, you'd think we were still sharing a womb.

I head right over to the sofa and start pulling the cushions off. "It's actually all your fault," I accuse, hoping he'll feel some responsibility for my idiocy and take it easy on me with all the laughter that is sure to ensue once he knows what I've been up to.

"Passing the buck is no way to garner my sympathy. Spill it."

So, I do. "Remember that Post-It with my number on it that I told you to give to Walter Junior?"

He shrugs.

"Well, it somehow wound up in the envelope with Aimée's pay. She assumed it was from you."

"So?"

"So, like every other young heterosexual woman who meets you, she's decided you would be the perfect addition to her friend collection."

I can see the wheels turning in my brother's head. His face morphs from confusion, to enlightenment, to utter hilarity in all of three seconds. "Hand me your phone," he orders.

There's no getting around it, so I do. He spends the next twenty minutes rereading Aimée's and my conversations out loud with much theatrical gusto. *Too much.*

After he's finally done—it's got to be nearly midnight—he gives me a brief recap. "You've got the hots for Aimée the sexy caterer, and you're wooing her—Cyrano de Bergerac -style—pretending to be me."

"In a nutshell, yes." I feel as low as the worm I am.

"Well, obviously, you can't keep doing that," he says while throwing his hands up in the air.

"Obviously."

Byron picks up my phone once again and types something in. Before I can ask what he's doing, he sticks one finger up in the air indicating that I should hold my horses. Then he hands me my phone and announces, "I'll be in charge from now on."

I read his text.

Me: Darling, I'm switching phones. Please text me on this number from now on. I have some wonderful ideas about how to get you and my boss together and I can't wait to share them with you.

"Byron, no! I don't have time to have the relationship with her that I want."

Getting into bed, my brother replies, "If that's the way you want it, I'll turn her on you so quickly she won't even be able to look at you."

I crawl under the covers silently. *Damn, that's not what I want either.*

Chapter Twenty-Five

Aimée

As much as I want to send Teisha to Fitzwilliam & Associates alone today, there's no way I can miss their first staff appreciation luncheon. I need to make sure things flow so smoothly that I'm their go-to caterer for the next decade, even if it does mean putting myself in the same room with my dream man.

Once again, I take great pains with my appearance. I need Noel to know exactly what he's passing up. I put on a petal pink A-line dress with a cinched waist that enhances my hourglass figure. Then I jazz up my makeup more than usual, tie my hair into a soft low ponytail, and slip my feet into some sexy high heels. *Eat your heart out, Mr. Fitzwilliam.*

Teisha walks by me and whistles. "Girl, you look like sex on a plate! Gonna get you some, huh?"

"Just trying to impress the client with my professionalism."

She gestures at my neckline and asks, "Is that what the kids are calling boobs these days?" Then she laughs. "Go get 'em tiger. I'm not judging you."

"Is it wrong that I want to make him sorry?"

"Honey"—she gives me one of her famous head waggles while making a Z with her pointer finger—"you wouldn't be normal if you didn't want him to suffer. I'm all aboard that train." Then she adds, "Put some flats on while we load up."

The van is fully packed by ten and we arrive at the Liberty Bank Building at a record eleven thirty. As soon as the elevator doors opens to the forty-second floor, Byron jumps to his feet and comes running. "Petal!" he calls out what I'm assuming is my new nickname.

I throw myself into his arms. "I've missed you!"

"Darling, I've missed you too, but now we're together again. Two peas in a pod! Two front teeth on a wee babe! Two bangers in a bun!"

Teisha interjects, "Two nuts in a shell …"

Byron shoots her an air kiss before helping us haul everything back to the kitchen. He sidles up to me and declares, "You look positively edible today. I could take a bite out of you!"

"What about your boss? Do you think he'll want to take a bite out of me?"

"I think he wants more than a bite," he says conspiratorially. "The object of this afternoon is to throw yourself at him while keeping your distance."

"I'm lost. How exactly do you envision me doing that?"

He stands back and mimes a performance like he's pretending to be me. He picks up a tray and sashays around the kitchen with such a hitch in his giddy-up I'm afraid he's going to dislocate a hip.

Then in a much higher voice, he leans over Teisha and asks, "Mr. Fitzwilliam, can I offer you a cocktail wiener?"

T lowers her voice and answers, "Only if I can offer you a jumbo frank in return." Then the two of them laugh and laugh like my sorry love life is the funniest thing in the world.

"Forget you guys," I yell. "This is not funny. I know I shouldn't be acting like I've broken up with the man I love, but cut me a break, will ya?"

"*Do* you love him?" Byron asks, sounding serious for the first time this morning.

Avoiding a direct answer, I say, "How could I possibly love him? It's not like it's you and we've been texting our deepest, darkest secrets." Then I shoot my new gay best friend my saddest puppy dog eyes and ask, "Are you sure you don't want to be straight for me?"

"If only it were possible for this leopard to change his spots, sweetheart. Alas, I'm a confirmed hot dog man, but don't give up hope. I think you and my persnickety boss still have a future."

Byron looks at the clock on the wall. "I'll leave you to it. Prepare to face the masses in T minus thirty minutes." Then he hurries out the door.

Teisha and I set up a variety of chafing dishes and platters that hold everything from soup to pasta to an assortment of sandwiches and salads. Cindy, of all people, is the first one to come in. She sidles up to me with a sneer on her face like a skunk just sprayed directly up her nose. "Is there anything that won't make me *fat*?" When she says "fat" she looks me up and down making it clear that she's calling me fat.

Teisha overhears, and offers, "I could pour you a nice glass of water if you'd like?" Her tone is so sickly sweet it's all I can do to keep from giggling.

"No, thank you." Then she looks at me and orders, "I'll have seven penne noodles and a large salad with no dressing. No cheese."

The buffet is set up for people to serve themselves so obviously there is some kind of power play afoot here. But I don't care, I'm making more today than I make in two weeks at the bakery. I pick up a plate and begin to serve her when Noel walks in. He takes the plate out of my hands and gives it to Cindy, before turning to me. "May I speak with you privately for a moment?"

I shoot T a look of panic before offering Cindy a smug smile. Then I answer him, "Of course." I follow him into his office like a lost puppy, or a sex-starved pirate, depending on how you look at it.

Noel shuts the door and gestures for me to sit in a chair across from his desk. Then he sits down and opens his desk drawer. "I think it would be easier for all if I went ahead and paid you for a month of lunches at once. I'm going to be extremely busy for the next several weeks, so I don't want to have to write more checks. How does that sound?"

"Good," I tell him while pushing my shoulders a little closer together and leaning forward to give him a better view of my assets. "Do you have any special requests?" My voice is all breathy like he just called 1-800-SEX-MEUP.

"I, um … well … yes … I …" *Oh, the power I feel!* "I like a good curry and I'm fond of bangers and mash." I give him a look that says, *everyone enjoys a good banger, do they?*

"How about Toad in the Hole or a nice Spotted Dick for dessert?" I don't know how sexy spotted dick sounds—it sounds like VD. Just let it be known, I'm not a pro at the sexy talk.

Noel doesn't seem to notice. He just answers, "Yes, to everything. I trust your culinary judgment explicitly." His eyes are still trained on my cleavage.

We both stop talking for several seconds, which feels kind of awkward. I decide to stand up and lean over his desk to give him a better show. "Can you make the check out to Nibbles and Noshes?"

That seems to snap him back to attention. "Wouldn't it be easier for you if I just made it out to you?"

"That's fine." I didn't suggest that because I didn't want him to think I wasn't totally professional. While he's writing the check, I ask, "Would you mind if I used your bathroom?"

"Um, er … no … not at all." I love how nervous he sounds. I make sure to follow Byron's example and glide slowly while adding a little shake to my money-maker. Then I look over my shoulder and offer Noel a smoldering glance before walking through the door. He is totally eating this up.

Once I'm inside, I check my lipstick in the mirror, make a couple of sexy faces to confirm that I've got it down, and then I proceed back out into the office. Noel isn't there. I walk over to the desk to find he's left me a check for a substantially larger amount than we agreed upon.

I hurry out of the office and stop at Byron's desk. "Where did he go?"

He looks up with mischief in his eyes. "Looks like the BM forgot an errand he had to run. He said he won't be back until lunch is over." At my crestfallen expression, he adds, "Don't pout, darling. Everything is going exactly to plan."

Chapter Twenty-Six

Noel

"You brought your snoozies to the office?" I ask Byron, pointing at his blue plaid slippers. He's paired them with a navy-blue satin pajama set and a gold eye mask that's currently resting just above his forehead.

"Uh, *yeah*," he answers, oozing sarcasm. "If I'm going to have to live here around the clock, I'm definitely bringing the comforts of home."

It's almost one in the morning and the thought of going home to my own bed instead of having another night with Byron the sleep-talker sounds extremely tempting. But since I need to be up in five hours to get back to work, I'll have to put up with it. He pulls a gold jacquard silk duvet and sheet set out of his giant Louis Vuitton suitcase (that he calls Big Louis) and starts making up the sofa bed. He smooths the duvet over the sheets, then returns to Big Louis and pulls out decorative pillows.

"I'm drawing the line at decorative pillows."

He glares at me, "I don't think you are, *Mr. Integrity*, because I'm pretty sure you need me to protect your big fat secret." Swiping his phone off the coffee table, he holds it up and gives me a smug smile. "Or should I text a certain caterer you're pretending not to love and tell her … well, anything I want, actually."

"You wouldn't."

"Remember the time you broke my CD player on purpose so I read your diary on the school's PA system?" he asks, his eyes wide with delight.

"This is hardly the same thing. They're pillows, for God's sake."

"Exactly," he says, carefully positioning them on the bed.

Rolling my eyes, I mutter, "Fine. Have it your way."

"You're just cranky because you want Aimée and you're too scared to go after her."

"Am not." I sigh and wave off his comment, then turn and reach into my duffle bag for a pair of sweats and a tee to sleep in.

"Yes, you are. I see the way you look at her. It must be how I look when I see a Stephen Curry ad for Degree body spray. You know, the *shirtless* ones?" He gets a faraway look in his eyes and I'm pretty sure I'll be blessed with a few minutes of silence while he mentally scrolls through his Stephen Curry photo files. I start to think I'm in the clear when he adds, "Exactly the same."

Damn. "Hardly," I say. "My relationship with Aimée is now and shall remain a professional one, my temporary lapse in judgment notwithstanding."

"Sigmund would have something to say about your lapse in judgment, you know?" he says, moving the useless pillows off his side of the bed and neatly stacking them on the coffee table before climbing in.

"Sigmund?"

"Freud, I assume you've heard of him …"

"And somehow you're on a first name basis with Dr. Freud?" I ask, raising one eyebrow.

"Don't try to distract me. You started texting her *for a reason*. Then you traveled like sixty-some blocks to a dingy basement spice shop *for a reason*. Then you offered her a regular gig, paid a huge dental bill for her—which is something you would never do for me, thank you very much—*for a reason*. And now, you expect me to believe it was all some random accident?" he asks, raising his voice. "You may be gullible enough to believe it, but I'm sure as heck not."

"It's really none of your business," I say, turning toward the bathroom. "I'm going to have a shower. Feel free to fall asleep before I get out."

"I might, or I might see if Aimée's up so we can talk about Sigmund …"

My gut tightens at the thought. "You got to use the pretty pillows. You can't go back on the deal now."

"That wasn't a deal. It was a threat."

"Well, your threat worked, now go to sleep already."

"I might, but not because you told me to. It's because I'm really tired," he says, tugging his eye mask over his eyes. "My git of a boss is running me ragged."

"And paying you well for it," I say, shutting the door behind me.

I use the power spray to work out my knotted neck muscles and, after a few minutes, find myself feeling slightly less cranky than I have all day. Although since Aimée used this shower, I can't help but imagine her in here, soaping up and washing her hair. That thought leads to me to one about her in that pink dress today, doing that thing with her chest that drained all the blood from my brain in under a second.

Nope. I am not going there. I am a hyper-focused professional on the precipice of greatness. My design legacy is imminent, and I'll soon join the greats like Zaha Hadid, Frank Lloyd Wright, and Renzo Piano. I'm going to think of nothing other than One Rosenthal for the next two-hundred and sixteen hours. And hopefully by then, I'll have forgotten all about Aimée, the beautiful caterer who tugs at my heartstrings. Hopefully, she will forget about me too. Because that's what will be best for her.

Even if I do end up spending the rest of my life going home to my empty apartment night after night, never knowing the comfort of having a wife to love …

Chapter Twenty-Seven

Aimée

AiméeT: You want to do what?! Please read that with the appropriate amount of alarm.

Byron: Don't be such a drama queen. All you have to do is tell Walter you want to meet for drinks at Bull Market here in our building. Then I'll lure Noel down there and he can see you on a date with someone else.

AiméeT: It's not like it's not a brilliant idea …

Byron: Then what's your problem?

AiméeT: It's just that I'm not some femme fatale and this definitely feels like a Mata Hari-level of machinations.

Byron: You don't need to impress me with big words. I'm already totally smitten. Plus, you had that sex goddess thing soooo down on Friday, I'm pretty sure Noel walked with a limp for two days.

AiméeT: What does that mean?

Byron: Oh, you sweet, innocent flower. It means it's easy to walk on two legs, but three is a little more difficult.

AiméeT: Byron, I'm shocked! But do you really think so? -smirk-

Byron: Affirmative, fair maiden. Yonder dragon is about to be slayed.

AiméeT: Okay, I'll tell him to be at Bull Market at seven.

Byron: Wear something that screams, "Take me now, Tarzan!"

AiméeT: I might have to go shopping.

Byron: Do it, and remember, tarts get more action.

AiméeT: I don't want Noel to think I look like a tart.

Byron: Like he'll even be able to think without any blood in his brain. Now go! Shop! Unleash your inner Eartha Kitt and purrrrrr, kitty!

AiméeT: Who's Eartha Kitt?

Byron: Just the most amazing Cat Woman who ever lived! You do know who Doris Day is, don't you? Before you say no, you should know our entire friendship is based on your saying yes.

AiméeT: Then of course I know who she is. Off to shop. I'll send pictures from the dressing room!

As soon as I get to the subway, I Google Doris Day. All I can say is, "Fabulous, much?" I feel a movie marathon with T and Byron coming up. I get out of the subway at Herald Square and plan to hit every department store within walking distance until I find the dress that will bring Noel to his knees.

I locate said creation at Macy's in the designer dress department, which I have no business being in. The prices are so shocking I almost talked myself out of the glorious creation I'm staring at in the dressing room mirror.

It's a simple black cocktail dress with a scoop neck and dropout back. There's a beaded fringe hem that flips and flops with every step like I'm a flapper from the twenties. On the hanger, the dress wasn't much to look at. In fact, I picked it up because I thought it looked classy, but on me? WOW! This thing hugs every one of my generous curves like a glove. I practice sitting in it, so I don't have another seam-splitting moment. I. Am. Yummy.

I snap a picture of myself and text it to both T and Byron. They both respond within seconds.

T: BUY IT NOW! The man doesn't stand a chance!

Byron: You know how I said there's no way I'd ever go for a girl. Well, honey, I felt a definite twitch in my trousers when I saw that picture. I don't care what it costs, that's the one.

I'm so giddy I'm practically popping out of my skin. I pay for the dress and then hurry down the street to Marcum where I made an appointment to have my hair and makeup done. I'm leaving nothing to chance.

Unfortunately, I get there to discover that some socialite walked in and took my appointment. "I was forty-seven seconds late," I complain to the snooty receptionist. "Which actually means I wasn't late because the minute hand hadn't moved yet."

She looks at me vacantly. "Carlos can see you after he's done with Mitzy."

After? After?! "I guess I'll have to wait then. What other choice do I have?" I sit down on the overstuffed hot-pink tufted stools and do the math on whether I can make it home and back downtown by seven. There's no way.

> AiméeT: My hair appointment got postponed and I won't have time to go home and change. What do I do?
>
> Byron: Don't be silly. Come up to my office and get ready here. I'll make sure the BM sees you and then he'll surely follow you down to the bar on his own accord.
>
> AiméeT: You're devious. Have I mentioned that I love you?
>
> Byron: You have, but you have my permission to say it again.
>
> AiméeT: I love you, Byron. You are the best!

After washing, trimming, and drying my hair, Carlos maneuvers it into a low french roll at the nape of my neck before releasing a few soft tendrils up. He loosens a couple more on either side to frame my face. "Soooooooooo sexy," he croons in an Italian accent. "You look freshly tumbled, yes?"

"Excuse me?" I ask, shocked while still absolutely appreciative of the compliment.

"Is that not the word?" He looks confused.

"No, no, I think it is."

He rotates the chair after taking the cape off my shoulders. "Gigi is waiting at the counter to do your makeup." As I walk away, I hear him say, "I pity the man who has to resist you."

Gigi is a six-foot four-inch black drag queen that I love on sight. After examining my face, she says, "I'm thinking smokey eyes with neutral skin tones and the barest hint of lipstick."

"I trust you fully," I tell her. And for some reason, I do.

"The idea is to give you that rolled in the hay look without actually coming in contact with hay." After performing her magic, Gigi turns me toward the mirror and says, "Sex kitten, party of one." I marvel that I'm really me. Once I put my dress on, I'm not sure I'll even recognize myself. After paying my bill and over-tipping the dream team of Carlos and Gigi, I walk back to the subway heading downtown to the Liberty Bank Building.

If the appreciative glances I receive are anything to go on, I look every bit as good as I think I do. By the time the elevator doors open, leading to Fitzwilliam & Associates, I'm feeling confident enough to take over the free world.

Byron takes one look at me and stands up from his desk and starts to applaud. "Mr. DeMille, your star is ready for her close up." Then he hurries toward me to grab my arm. Pulling me in the direction of Noel's office, he says, "His Highness stepped out for a minute. Go change into your dress in his bathroom. I cannot wait to see the final product!"

Back in Noel's bathroom, I feel like I've come full circle since the day I was forced to wear Cindy's tiny wet pants. Once the dress is on, I slip on a pair of knock-off Jimmy Choos I bought because I didn't have time to go home and get my own shoes. This day has cost me a fortune, but one glance in the long mirror behind the bathroom door tells me that it was worth every single penny and then some.

Temporarily leaving my things in the bathroom, I hurry out to show Byron how I look. But it isn't Byron I see. No, sir. Once again, I fly straight into the arms of Noel Fitzwilliam. The look on his face is one of priceless awe. When he doesn't move me out of his arms, or say anything for that matter, I offer, "Noel. How are you?"

"Aimée?" His tone is rife with his shock, disbelief, and appreciation.

"Yes."

"What are you doing here?"

"Oh, sorry about that. Byron told me I could use your office to get ready."

"What are you getting ready for?" he demands.

"I have a date tonight and I didn't have time to go home and change. Byron told me to come here."

"I just bet he did," he says in a low growl before adding, "What date?"

Smiling prettily, if not smugly, I answer, "I'm meeting Walter Junior for drinks downstairs at Bull Market."

"The hell you are." He pulls me even closer like he's trying to protect me from a mauling.

I push him away. "Actually, I am. You don't have any objections about me going out on a date, do you?"

His face turns so red I'm half expecting his head to blow off like a cartoon character's. Schooling his expression, he manages, "No, of course not. I just think you can do a lot better than Walter Junior."

"I'm not sure I can," I say, knowing full well that'll make him mad. "Not only is he a real gentleman, he's handsome, and he's an upstanding member of the real estate development community. Plus, if he's good enough for you to do business with, surely, he's good enough to date your caterer."

Noel runs his tongue over his teeth, then says, "In my experience, the best businessmen make lousy boyfriends. I suspect that would be the case with Junior." He adds a little extra emphasis on Junior.

"So don't date him." I look at my wrist even though I'm not wearing a watch and add, "I'd better get going. I don't want to keep him waiting."

With those words, I sway my hips right on out of his office.

Chapter Twenty-Eight

Noel

Standing in the doorway to my office, watching Aimée make her way to the elevator, is excruciating. Especially when she stops to give Byron a tight hug that he most certainly does not deserve. That dress with the fringe? She could be a stand-in for Marilyn Monroe in *Some Like it Hot*. She looks so delectable I'm actually biting my knuckles. Who does that outside of bad television shows? Me, apparently.

After Aimée steps onto the elevator, the doors close, and she's presumably whisked down to the main floor where Walter the Wanker is likely rubbing his hands together in anticipation like some Three-penny Opera villain. Shaking my head, I go back to my desk. Anything that is happening outside this office tonight is none of my concern. I need to stay the course and get back to work. People are depending on me.

After grabbing my laptop, I trudge to the conference room where the team is waiting. The wall of windows overlooking the East River serves as a crappy reminder that it's well past quitting time.

That's somehow made harder by the fact that it's a warm spring evening. I take my usual spot at the head of the table and try to get my brain in the game.

Byron looks over at me and puts on his most innocent expression. "Hey boss, would you like me to run out and get dinner for everyone? Maybe some of Bull Market's famous sliders?"

Not only does the bastard know what he's doing, he knows *I* know what he's doing. I glare daggers at him, refocusing every ounce of the frustration pouring through me after seeing Aimée in that dress.

Cindy, who's leaning her cheek on her arm with her eyes closed, mumbles, "I'll have a side salad, hold the dressing."

"Cheeseburger and sweet potato fries," Jack groans while holding up his hand like he's in primary school.

Byron starts to write down everyone's orders when I stand up. "Forget it. Everybody go home."

The room goes dead quiet.

"Take the night off. We're all exhausted. We can get a fresh start tomorrow morning. Just be here by seven."

"Really?" Ali bolts out of his chair like I just announced free college tuition for four to the first person on the elevator.

Nodding my head to their retreating forms, I say, "Really, you've more than earned it. Now get out of here." Of course, most of them are already gone.

I'm left alone with my brother. Byron asks, "So, no sleepover tonight?"

"Pack up Big Louis and go home," I tell him, gesturing with my head to the door.

His smile is so toothy, it threatens to take over his entire face. "Mmm hmm ... I knew it."

"Don't start," I say, while standing up and collecting the papers in front of me.

Byron follows me down the hall. "You like her. You like her so much you can't *stand* the idea that she's on a date with some other guy—a rather handsome, not to mention rich as sin one, I might add. They're downstairs in this very building at this exact moment, while you're up here pretending to be a martyr."

"A martyr? That's pretty dramatic, Byron."

He points to the ceiling. "You're up there hanging on the cross acting like you're too important to the world to be normal and accept a little companionship in your life."

"Don't be ridiculous," I tell him.

"You're going to go down there, aren't you? As soon as I'm gone, you're going to go and spy on them."

I audibly scoff at the idea, even though that's exactly what I want to do. "I'm going to order something to be delivered and I'm going to get back to work. I'll see you in the morning," I say, while mock saluting him. If he doesn't move fast, I'm going repeat the gesture with my foot to his backside.

Tilting his head from side to side, Byron says, "You're consumed by jealousy, I can tell. This is the same look you had when Penelope Smythe invited *me* to her knickers and kickers World-Cup party and not you."

"For your information, I am *not* a ball of jealous rage," I tell him with my jaw clenched so tightly it actually hurts. I continue to lie, "That gorgeous woman who just sashayed out of here to go on a date with a complete tosser—the one who's probably going to treat her like a prostitute—means nothing to me outside of her culinary acumen." Am I raising my voice? I think I am. Clearing my throat, I add, "If you're so worried about her, maybe you should go down and play chaperone in case Walter comes on too strong."

Byron folds his arms across his chest. "You lost her and you know it. It hurts like a cricket bat to the bollocks, doesn't it? I don't feel sorry for you though. You brought this upon yourself."

My shoulders drop and I let out a long, frustrated breath. "Just go home, Byron. Before I change my mind and make you stay. I've got another five hours of work in me, and nothing would please me more than causing you another night of lost sleep."

"Fine. I'll go." He narrows his eyes like he's examining a slug under a microscope. "But I'm not going to spy on Aimée and her date. I trust she knows how to take care of herself." Picking up Big Louis, he adds, "I'm going home to have a long, hot bath and wait for Aimée to text me. I told her to let me know how he *is* …"

"Small," I mutter, turning from him and making my way over to my desk.

My brother offers his parting shot. "Sometimes small is better than nothing. At least she's getting herself some."

Pointing to the door, I yell, "Out!"

After Byron goes, I replay the texting session with Aimée where she told me (when she thought I was Byron) that she was going to give Walter Junior fifth date privileges tonight as a way to rebuild her flagging self-esteem. The same self-esteem I shat all over by turning down her advances. Maybe I should just head down to Bull Market and grab a bite to go.

The longer I sit in my office attempting to reconfigure the cross-ventilation in what will become a four-story atrium, the clammier my hands become. Knowing Aimée is down there in that dress with that dickwit is making it impossible for me to concentrate. Especially as it doesn't take a psychic to predict what Walter has in mind.

And it's not marrying her.

Chapter Twenty-Nine

Aimée

I spot Walter as soon as I walk into Bull Market, which turns out to be an impressively upscale establishment catering to Wall Street types. My date doesn't see me yet, which is good because he appears to be hitting on a Cindy-clone. It's not her though, thank God.

When I'm fewer than ten feet away, I see him slide his business card across the bar to her before leaning in and whispering something. I can't hear what he says, but I'm a thousand percent certain he's not suggesting a business meeting. Gross.

I would turn around and walk out of here right now if I wasn't hoping with all of my heart for Noel to show up. Forcing a smile, I tap Walter on the shoulder. "Hey, I hope you haven't been waiting long."

He startles and turns around. Standing up, he slams back whatever that amber liquid is sitting in the glass in front of him. "Aimée, hello! I was just talking to my friend ..." he gestures toward his barstool companion to fill in the blank. They're obviously so close he doesn't know her name.

Instead of playing along and pretending to be his buddy, she blows him a kiss before eyeing me up and down. "Call me," she purrs. Then she turns her back on us. She's either a high-class call girl—oxymoron, party of one—or she's looking for a casual hookup and Walter Junior is ticking all of her boxes.

"Let's go find a booth," Walter says, while sliding his hand around my waist in a proprietary fashion. An involuntary shudder of disgust shoots through my nervous system. After sitting down, I expect him to take the seat across from me, but he doesn't. He scoots in right after me like he's trying to make room for a third person. He's practically on top of me.

Walter flags down a cocktail waitress and lifts his empty tumbler, "Two more of these."

"I prefer a glass of wine," I tell him.

He looks back at the waitress. "Two more of these for me and a glass of the house white for my friend." I start to wonder how many cocktails Walter had before I got here. He must be a serious drinker to order them two at a time.

As soon as our waitress leaves, I ask, "Walter, would you mind moving? I need to use the ladies'." It's a good thing I don't really have to go because he takes his sweet time. When he does get up, I practically sprint to freedom. Once I'm safely in the restroom, I have to resist the urge to give myself a bath in the sink to wash off the creepy crawlies. Instead, I lock myself in a stall. Pulling out my phone, I text Byron.

AiméeT: If Noel isn't down here in ten minutes, I'm out. Walter Junior is a disgusting pig.

Byron: Oh no, what happened?

AiméeT: He was hitting on another woman when I got here, he's already pretty tipsy, and he isn't acting like he's ever heard of the term "personal space."

Byron: I'm in the lobby, do you want me to come to your rescue?

AiméeT: No, just get Noel down here.

Byron: I'll text him that I just heard from you. I'll tell him things are going so well you're planning on taking your date up to Walter's place. That ought to move him along.

AiméeT: Hurry!

After signing off with Byron, I leave the bathroom and stand out of sight of my date until I can flag our waitress down. She comes over as soon as she sees me. "Can you please replace my wine with sparkling water? I don't want my date to know I'm not drinking."

"He'll know when I bring the bill," she tells me.

"Not if you charge him for wine." I share a conspiratorial look with her before adding, "I think you should charge a higher price than the house, though. What a cheapskate."

I pull a twenty out of my wallet and hand it to her. "This is for you. I'm guessing the guy I'm here with isn't a big tipper unless he's hoping to buy other privileges."

Pocketing the money, she says. "I know the type. Thanks for taking care of me."

"I'm a waitress too," I tell her. "I know how horrible people can be."

With a shocked expression, she asks, "What are you doing down here with him?"

"It's a long story."

"Well, come back and tell me sometime. I'd like to hear it." With a wave, she walks off.

When I get back to the table, I sit across from Walter hoping he takes the hint. He doesn't, He gets up and moves in next to me. Then he leans in and slurs, "What took you so schlong? I missed you." *Oh, for the love of God, how is this a successful businessman?*

"I'm here now," I tell him, hoping I don't sound as disgusted as I feel. I need him to think I'm into this as much as he is, at least until Noel arrives. I spread my knees slightly to force him to move over.

"The minute I saw you at that meeting at Fitzwilliam I couldn't think about anything else but getting you into bed."

Ew. "Really? You weren't thinking about the pitch?" I'm offended on Noel's behalf. I know how hard his whole staff has worked on that for an entire year.

"Nah. We were always going to give the project to Lassiter and Sons. We just needed to make it look like we were considering other offers in the spirit of fair play."

Fair play, my Aunt Fanny! Who uses an entire firm like that with no intention of taking their bid seriously? "Are you still going with Lassiter?" I ask innocently. I can't tip him off that I know all about Noel killing himself to make changes to his original design.

"That's the pisser," he says while slamming his leg into mine so he can scoot closer. "Lassiter had a sure thing. All they had to do was give us what we asked for. After a closer look at their bid, we started to see discrepancies in the quality of material we specified. It spooked us into thinking they were trying to set things up to skim off the top. That's a deal breaker for us."

The waitress appears to take our orders, shooting me an "are you all right?" look and I give her a slight eye-roll that shows I'm okay but not happy.

Walter orders for me. "I thought we'd just have appies—I know how much you ladies *love* to share food." He bites the air at me as if he thinks he's a sexy lion. Turning back to the waitress, he orders the three-appetizer special—fries, dry ribs, and edamame beans. Classy guy.

The waitress looks at me and says, "I'll have these out in record time."

My completely oblivious date replies, "Noice."

When she leaves, I get right back to asking about the project. "So you really are considering

Noe... I mean, Fitzwilliam & Associates?" I hope he didn't catch my slip of almost saying Noel's name.

"The job is theirs as long as they don't mess it up like Lassiter did." Walter runs his sticky fingers across my mouth in a way I'm pretty sure he thinks is seductive.

I shift a little in my seat and start asking about a topic I know will distract him—*him*. I stall for time, pretending I'm incredibly interested in yacht racing and his boa constrictor (real, not metaphorical, but most likely an attempt at compensating for something).

The food arrives and Walter picks up a fry, dipping it in the sauce that's meant for the ribs, and attempts to feed me. I snatch it out of his hand and pop it in my mouth myself, then ask him about how he decided to enter into his family business.

"Let's not talk about the past. I'm much more interested in the future—like what I want to do to you after we get out of here."

It's all I can do not to puke on his hand. *Does this crap work with other women?* My eyes scan around the room, frantically hoping to see Noel. Like the sun breaking through a stormy sky, I spot him at the bar. Hallelujah!

Leaning into Walter, I say, "I'm not planning on going home with you. I don't do anything like that on a first date."

"Let's pretend that lunch you catered for my office was our first date then. You know the lunch I paid you a pretty penny for?"

I actually gag at his words before picking up my sparkling water and slamming it back like I'm playing a drinking game in college. "You mean the lunch I catered at market rate? The one you didn't tip on?"

"I've got your tip right here, baby," he says before sticking out his tongue and licking my ear. If that wasn't gross enough, the smell of his breath is enough to knock me over.

I peek up and see Noel sitting at the bar, staring straight at us. It's now or never. I either have to look like I'm fending off an attack, or make it appear like I'm enjoying Walter's advance. I decide to go for the honest approach.

Pushing Walter away, I say. "I would rather have my arm chewed off by an alligator than be on this date for one more minute."

"You like it rough, do you?" This man is oblivious to how revolting he is.

"Yeah, Walter. I like it rough. Rough like tying you up before setting you on fire."

"Oh, baby, I'm on fire all right." Before I know it, he's practically on top of me. I'm about to scream for real when I look up and see Noel standing in front of us.

Chapter Thirty

Noel

Forty minutes earlier ...

I am not proud of what I'm doing. Repeat—*not proud*.

Sitting at a corner stool in the very busy Bull Market, sipping a coffee whilst waiting for my to-go order, reeks of stalker-type behavior. It goes so far beyond any reasonable action of any reasonable person that I can't even see the line I crossed. But *come on*, Walter Freaking Junior? I don't think so.

Aimée can do so much better, even if she doesn't believe it. She just needs a few more weeks of Byron-style ego boosting and she'll be off and running to find a man that will be exactly right for her. Why does that thought feel like a sucker-punch to the gut?

"Are you done with that?" the beefy bartender asks, gesturing to the menu I've been pretending to peruse while I keep an eye on the two of them in a red leather booth on the far side of the bar.

"What?" I ask, feeling my face heat up.

"The menu," he says slowly. "You already ordered so I was wondering if you're done with it. We have other customers, you know."

"Not quite yet ..." I glance down at his name tag. *Arnold*. Fitting because he looks like Conan the Barbarian, only in a golf shirt and jeans. "I may order dessert."

He shakes his head and walks away, leaving me to my stalking.

The longer I sit here, the worse I feel. Because Aimée actually looks like she's having a nice time. She certainly is laughing a lot anyway. Gross. Walter just slid closer to her in the booth, and now he's dipping a chip into some sort of sauce and trying to feed it to her.

Good for her for not letting him. "Ha! I knew she couldn't like that tosser."

"Sorry?" Arnold asks, leaning down in a way that's slightly menacing. "Did you just call me a tosser?"

"No," I say. "I would never do that. I was considering having a tossed salad. Back in England we call them tossers. I'll have a tosser, thank you," I say putting on an extra-English accent for some reason.

"I think maybe you should leave."

Bollocks. "I was serious. I would like a tossed salad with a balsamic vinaigrette dressing. Please. And some dessert." I make a clicking sound. "I'll need a few minutes to decide on which one though. So many tempting options."

Lucky for me, a couple of women seat themselves a few stools over and start waving to get

Arnie's attention. That should keep him busy for a while. Back to Aimée's date. Yuck. Walter is tracing her collar bone with one finger and … sniffing her neck? Who does he think that crap works on?

My girl is clearly not having it because she just reaches out with the arm closest to him and picks up her wine glass, subtly shrugging him off. You show him, Aimée!

Just don't overdo it on the wine, love. My phone buzzes in my suit jacket pocket and I slide it out while still keeping watch. I glance at it quickly. It's Byron. When I answer, he says, "How's their date going?"

"How would I know?"

"Because you're sitting at the bar watching them."

"Am not. I'm in the office." *How dare he?*

"Then why does your office sound exactly like a trendy restaurant?"

Dammit. "I've got the telly on."

"I'm your twin, you idiot. I know you better than I know myself. You lasted about two minutes after my text, then you told yourself you were just going to order take away and have a quick peek to make sure everything's fine. Now you're likely hiding behind a pillar like Inspector Clouseau hot on a case."

"I'm hiding behind a menu," I say, knowing when I'm beaten. "They don't have pillars in here."

"So back to my first question. How's the date going?"

"Disgusting. He's sniffing her like a pig searching for truffles. Also, I'm a little worried she's drinking too much wine—which in her case is a terrible idea. Text her and tell her to stick to one glass, okay?"

"I'll do no such thing. She's a grown woman. She can drink as much as she likes."

"Well, *you* haven't seen her after three glasses of wine. She's like 'Me So Horny' by 2 Live Crew. Why exactly did you call, Byron?"

"To help you."

"Why do you think I need your help?" I ask, watching as the waitress brings her another glass of wine. Son of a …

"Because you're doing something rather risky at the moment, and you're not particularly skilled at risky endeavors."

"Please, I'm a veritable 007 when faced with peril."

"Uh-huh. Remember the time you tried to toilet paper your Latin teacher's house? You nearly got it done before you panicked and started taking it all down."

"I felt bad. He had arthritis."

"Yes, well, it was the clean-up that got you caught. If you had just run away, you never would have been hauled down to the police station."

"I was *eleven*," I hiss. "I assure you I've gotten a bit better at handling high-pressure situations over the last twenty-five years."

"Are you saying you've already come up with a plan should you get caught spying on your caterer and your most important client?"

"I'm carefully hidden."

"What if Walter Junior turns out to be the rapey type?"

I'm guessing that's a pretty accurate assessment, given what I'm seeing. "I can easily make up some sort of catering emergency to get her out of here, should the need arise."

"Just make sure you don't overreact and inject yourself in a situation where you're not wanted," he says.

"If you were so worried I'd do that, why the bloody hell did you set me up like this?" I ask, raising my voice to a level that earns me a warning look from Arnold.

"Because I'm a romantic," he says. "And I want to see you happy. Aimée would make you happy. But, when I got home, I realized what's at stake for the company and I got a little worried."

"Well, don't. I've got it covered. And I'm not here so I can have her for myself. I'm here so she won't make a mistake with a guy who's not fit to clean the dirt off her shoes."

"I'm going to hang up now, but I want you to think hard about what you just said, mmkay?"

I growl and put my phone on silent so I can stalk in peace.

"Here you go," Arnold says, handing me a thick brown paper bag with my order. "That'll be thirty-six ninety."

I look up at him. "Oh, I think I will get the um …" I look at the desserts for the first time. Oh, they have a chocolate lava cake that takes twenty minutes to bake. "Lava cake, please."

He gives me a deadpan expression, then reaches over and yanks the menu from my hands. "Dude, are you serious?" He walks away in a huff like he's offended by my love of lava cake.

Crouching behind my to-go bag, I briefly wonder if I should cut eye holes in it.

Probably not.

Before my dessert even arrives, Arnold hands me a check. "Forty-eight ninety-five. You can pay this now."

"Righto," I say, reaching in my pocket for my wallet whilst watching Walter drape his arm over Aimée's shoulder and proceed to lick her ear. I throw my credit card at Arnold without even looking.

"This is a Hilton points card, man. Come on, it's a busy night. I don't have time for this."

I hand my entire wallet over to him. "Just pick one."

Aimée looks like she's trying to act nonchalant, but she's definitely scooting her bottom away from Walter. He pulls her back with one hand as his other disappears under the table.

"All right, that's it!" I shout, standing up suddenly.

I can feel the eyes of people around me, but I don't care. I stride over to their booth at a furious pace, weaving through tables and dodging servers with absolutely no clue as to what I'm going to say when I get over there.

When I do arrive, I clear my throat loudly, then just stare, waiting for my brain to catch up with the moment.

"Noel," they both say at that same time. Walter looks annoyed, but Aimée's eyes reflect pure relief.

"Yes, it's me," I say with a firm nod. "I'm glad I caught you, Aimée. I was upstairs working on …" Turning to Walter, I say, "One Rosenthal, obviously. Coming along beautifully, I might add." Then, looking back at Aimée, I announce, "Your roommate called looking for you. She was hoping you were still at the office. Her um … gran died. Toppled off a cliff at Niagara Falls, if you can believe it."

"Oh, my god," Aimée says, putting on a concerned expression. "Poor Teisha."

"Tragic really. Apparently she'd waited her whole life just to see the falls, only to …" I make a motion of falling off a cliff with one hand. "Fall off it."

"Are you serious?" Walter grumbles. I can tell he is not buying it.

"Teisha, that dear lamb, is quite upset," I say, shaking my head gravely. "Sobbing uncontrollably. Took the poor girl nearly ten minutes to tell me what happened."

Aimée looks at Walter. "I'm so sorry, but I should go to her."

Walter clenches his jaw, then throws up his hands.

Just as Aimée starts to scoot out of the booth and I begin to think I'm in the clear, Arnold taps me on the shoulder. "Here's your wallet, meal, and dessert."

Walter raises one eyebrow at me, and I turn to Arnold. "You must have me confused with someone else. I didn't order food. I wouldn't have had time because I just came in to give my colleague here some bad news."

"Really?" Arnold asks, glaring at me from under his thick eyebrows. "So you're not the same guy who was sitting at the bar hiding behind the menu for the last forty minutes? Because you're a dead ringer for him."

"I have one of those faces, I'm afraid," I say with a nervous chuckle.

"Right. Okay, well I'll just go throw out this food and put your wallet in lost and found."

Nuts. "Oh, that is my wallet," I say, plucking it out of his enormous hand. Then to Aimée, I say, "Must have dropped that in my hurry to find you."

She's trying valiantly not to laugh.

"I told Teisha I'd get you home straight away, so we should ..." I gesture to the entrance with my head.

"Yeah, we better go," Aimée says. "Bye, Walter. Thanks for dinner."

Crap. One look at Walter's face has me wondering if I should call a halt to our attempt at winning the bid on One Rosenthal.

Chapter Thirty-One

Aimée

"Are you all right?" Noel asks as soon as we step into the lobby of the building.

"I could use a shower to get the Walter off me, but otherwise, I'm fine," I say, turning to him. "Thank you, by the way."

"Think nothing of it." He takes my hand and moves us in the direction of the elevators instead of the exit.

My hand fits perfectly in his—like it was meant to be held by this man and no other. I want to kiss him. So. Badly. It. Hurts. But then I remember he's not available and never will be and I start to feel irritation bubbling up in my empty stomach. "Why did you really come down here?" I ask.

"I was hungry, and Bull Market was handy."

"Yet you walked out of there without your food," I tell him.

The elevator doors open. He lets go of my hand and presses his fingertips on the small of my back to usher me inside. The heat warms my entire body, starting at my core and spreading through to my toes and up to my cheeks.

We stand beside each other, shoulders touching as we start our ascent. Noel glances down at me, then looks straight ahead. "Look, I know it was wildly inappropriate and utterly unacceptable for me to be ... watching you on a date, but the thing is, I know Walter's type. Total vermin as far as women are concerned. And from what I saw, I wasn't wrong to worry."

I bite my bottom lip as the evening's events play out in my mind. "I should have seen it coming. I don't know what I was thinking," I say. "What a waste of a new dress."

"That dress ..." he says in a low tone.

Oh, that voice. That accent. That's it. I'm done waiting for him to make the first honest move between us. I know he wants me as much as I want him and someone has got to get the ball rolling. I turn toward him, essentially pinning him between me and the wall. "I can't figure you out. You say you're not interested, and yet everything you do says the opposite. If I'm nothing to you, why would you go to all that trouble—especially when you should be working."

He glances down at my lips. "I felt responsible for introducing you to Walter in the first place."

"I don't believe you," I say in a breathy tone. "I think there's some other reason, but you're not willing to admit it."

He lowers his head toward mine and murmurs, "It's because you deserve so much better."

He leans down a little more and grazes my neck with his lips. Unlike when Walter was digging his face into my neck and sniffing me like I was a dog's behind, I'm totally on board with this. I don't say anything though. I don't want to break the mood. "Oh God, you smell so good," Noel groans.

He continues to hold me against him—hello, he's not as indifferent to me as he'd like me to believe—until the elevator opens up again. Suddenly, it's like the spell we were under is lifted and reality floods in with the bright lights from his office. Noel sighs, closing his eyes and taking his hands off me. "You deserve someone who will be there for you, not someone who stays late at the office every night." I take a step back, leaving an empty space between us, then turn and walk toward his office. "Right. I forgot you're the only person on the planet who runs his own business. I guess I should get my things and go home."

I hurry past him to the bathroom to collect my change of clothes. When I walk out, he's rubbing the back of his neck with a tortured look on his face. Good. He should feel conflicted. He's been conflicting the hell out of me for weeks.

"Wait. Please stay," he says, then quickly adds, "You didn't really get a chance to eat, and to go home now would be a total waste of that dress." He gives me a very sexy smile, but I don't return it. "Maybe we could order in like we did the other night, only with less wine?"

He looks so desperate to keep me here I don't have the heart to yell at him for toying with me, even though I'm sorely tempted to. I stare at him for a long moment, wanting nothing more than to stay, but then I shake my head. "Unless you've suddenly changed your mind about things, I don't think that's a good idea," I tell him honestly. "If I sit here with you and pretend you mean nothing to me, I'll only be hurting myself."

He runs his fingers through his hair. "I wish I could make you understand. My life is … not really my own. I have so many people relying on me, I just don't have time for a personal life."

"That's totally your call," I tell him. "You've made it perfectly clear how you feel, so I don't think there's any point in continuing a flirtation when nothing can come of it. I hope we can still be business associates, though." Because, dear God, I really do need the job.

"Of course. I'm not such a cad that I'd make our work relationship dependent on you know …"— he points to himself and then to me—"something happening here."

"Good. That speaks well of you, at least."

"I'll call you a car." He walks over to his desk and picks up his phone, then orders a car. When he hangs up, he says, "It'll be ten minutes. I'll walk you out."

I sigh and press my tongue against my top teeth. "Why do you have to do that?"

"Do what?"

"Be so … perfect all the time," I spit out, waving my hand to gesture to his entire body. Imitating him, I say, " 'I'll walk you out.' You're such a tease."

He blinks in surprise. "I've never been called that before."

"Maybe not to your face."

"The last thing I want to do is frustrate you. I'm just trying to be a man of honor. I'd never want to turn any woman into a work-widow, especially not someone like you."

"Oh, my God!" I shout. "Do you think this is the eighteenth century? Do you think I'm just going to sit at home doing needlepoint, waiting for your arrival at the end of each day? In case you haven't noticed, I have my own hopes and dreams—big, juicy ones that mean I won't have that much time for you, either. But I'm not just going to throw in the towel on love and say, 'oh well, I guess I can't ever have a relationship because I want to run an incredibly popular catering business and make piles of money!'"

"Aimée—"

"I'm not done yet," I say, throwing my balled-up clothes on the floor and stepping right up to him, breathing hard with rage. "People do this all the time. They have careers *and* relationships. They … they hang out together on the couch while they're both working on their laptops. They kiss each other goodbye early in the morning, happy that they'll have someone to come home to at the end of a long day. They support each other and talk about things that they're proud of or scared of, or even angry about. It can work, you moron! It literally works for millions of people all over America every damn day!"

Noel pulls me into his arms and lifts me up until my feet are practically off the ground. Then he kisses me like his life depends on it. And oh, wow, it's the kiss of a lifetime. The greatest kiss I've ever had—it somehow weakens my knees and makes me feel incredibly powerful at the same time. I wrap my hands around his neck and pull him to me, pressing myself against him, as close as two fully-dressed people can be. His hands are on my cheeks now as his tongue and mine do the most delicious things to each other. It's the perfect blend of spicy and sweet and I'm so caught up in it, I don't care what happens tomorrow. I just don't want this to stop.

He pulls back and rests his forehead against mine, his breath ragged on my skin. "Oh God, Aimée … I want you so badly. You do something to me, something amazing and wonderful and terrifying all at the same time. I've broken all of my rules for you. And no matter how much I tell myself to forget about you, I can't. I just can't."

He kisses me again urgently, showing me how much he wants me. His hands move down to my bottom and he squeezes firmly, then lifts me off the floor. I wrap my legs around his waist wishing we were not dressed because this is the sexiest moment of my whole life. He walks over to his desk and sets me down on it, and the two of us start to fumble with each other's clothes. I lift the bottom of his shirt out of his pants and put my hands under the fabric, feeling the heat of his hard body while he unzips my dress and slips it off my shoulders.

The phone rings, intruding at the worst moment possible. Well, maybe not the worst …

Noel pulls back and says, "That'll be your car. Do you still want to go?"

I shake my head and kiss him again, unable to articulate with words.

He reaches over and fumbles for the receiver, picking it up while our lips are still glued together, pulling back just long enough to say, "Thanks, but I won't be needing the car after all."

Then he slams the receiver down. I can tell by the look on his face, this is going to be well worth the wait.

Chapter Thirty-Two

Noel
Three weeks later ...

"Mmm ..." I moan as the savory blend of flavors and the light pastry of the chicken vol-au-vent dance across my tongue. "So, so good," I murmur, forking another bite.

We're at my place and Aimée's been hard at work testing out new recipes for a big gig she's got in a couple of days. I'm putting the finishing touches on our presentation redo for the Walters tomorrow. After Aimée and I had our first night together, she told me that Junior had let it slip that unless we screwed up in a massive way, the job was ours. Once I heard that, I decided to make seven p.m. the very latest anyone would have to stay at the office until we got the design wrapped up. I owe my team big and the first payoff is going back to semi-reasonable hours. The next payoff will be a sizable bonus in their paychecks once we sign on the dotted line for One Rosenthal.

The added benefit has been allowing me to have what Aimée calls a "balanced" life. She's totally right, too because the last three weeks have been pure heaven. She's stayed over every night and although we don't get much sleep, I've never had more energy. Who knew waking up with the same woman every day could be so ... amazing? Certainly not me.

"So I should add it to the rotation?" she asks, grinning at me as I practically lick the plate clean.

"You'd be crazy not to," I say, leaning over and giving her a lingering kiss that says I'm in the mood for something other than food.

She kisses me back and I pull her onto my lap. After a few very delightful moments, she pulls back and gets up suddenly. "No way. You've got to finish that," she says, pointing to my computer. "And I need to clean up. I've made a huge mess in my boyfriend's kitchen, and I don't know if you know this about him, but he's a bit of a neat freak."

"Am not," I say, narrowing my eyes in mock irritation. "I just like things a certain way for the aesthetics of it. Things just flow better and feel calmer when they're clean and organized."

She glances at me, giving me a sideways grin. "But you're not a neat freak."

"You know, a lot of women would kill for a guy who doesn't leave his socks and underpants all over the floor ..." I say, staring at my laptop again and trying to remember what I was doing before the most welcome interruption. "Someone who puts the cap on the toothpaste when he's done ... the kind of guy who'd book a cabin in Vermont for this weekend so he can whisk his girlfriend off and do very naughty things to her in a rural setting."

Aimée lets out a loud whoop, then rushes over, grabbing my cheeks with her soapy wet hands.

She plants a huge kiss on me before saying, "You are going to get so lucky, mister."

I kiss her back, then wipe the suds off my face. "I already have. I finally got you to go out with me."

As soon as she's safely back on the other side of the island, I add, "As impossible a task as that was. Honestly, why you thought this couldn't work beyond me. It was so obvious we were made for each other."

Oh, that did it. I quickly shut my laptop because now she's racing at me with a wild look in her eyes and I know I'm in for it. I spring out of my chair and run to the bedroom with her in hot pursuit. I turn around just in time for her to launch herself at me, causing both of us to land on the bed with me pinned underneath her. "I win," I say with a smirk.

"You win? I won," she says, looking adorably sexy and frustrated at the same time.

"Nope, I win. I got you into the bedroom, which was my objective all along."

"You were running like a scared little girl," she says, lowering her mouth over mine.

With a quick flip, I'm on top of her, pressing myself against her and kissing her neck. "Do I seem like a scared little girl now?"

Bursting out laughing, Aimée says, "Maybe let me do the sexy talk from now on."

I chuckle and nod. "That might work better."

"Shut up and take your clothes off."

"Gladly."

Chapter Thirty-Three

Aimée

I'm whistling vintage Spice Girls songs to myself while walking down Amsterdam Avenue like I haven't a care in this world. I have the sweetest, sexiest, most adorable boyfriend on the planet, and even though we've only been seeing each other for three weeks, this morning I told him I loved him.

Lying in bed, Noel regaled me with stories about his horrible stuffy parents. I told him about my sweet and loving ones. He wanted to know how two people from such different backgrounds could be as good together as we are. I explained that love knew no boundaries. That's when he pulled me toward him and held on tight. "Are you saying what I think you're saying?"

"I love you, Noel Fitzwilliam, and I don't mean maybe."

The best part? He said it back. And we didn't get up for another hour, even though he's got his big presentation today. I sent him off to work with a big kiss and two trays of baked goods (with lots of extra cookies for Walter Senior). Since it'll be much shorter than their first meeting, they didn't think a full lunch was needed.

As I near Bean Town, I spot no fewer than eight dogs tied up to a bike rack. That means Jen is here. T and I have been friendly with her ever since she started coming into the bakery. In the last few months, we've upped that relationship to genuine friendship. We even give her bags of day-old pastries to she can keep herself fed while saving money to buy more paint and canvases. My knowledge of the art world may be limited, but I know enough to realize she's enormously talented.

I stop to pet a couple of her charges before walking inside. I gave my notice at Bean Town two weeks ago. Between jobs at Noel's and a few others that have started cropping up as a result, I've been too busy to work here. I've been suffering scone withdrawal something fierce.

Being that Dr. Pearlman is putting my permanent crown on this afternoon, I figured I'd reward myself with a currant scone beforehand. Also, I haven't seen Teisha in days and I miss her.

Walking into Bean Town, I look around until I see T and Jen. They're sitting at a small table by the window. When my roomie spots me, she cocks her head to the side while tapping her cheek. "Does that girl remind you of someone, Jen?"

Jen plays right along. "Kind of. But the girl I'm thinking of fell off of the face of the earth. There's no way it can be her."

I open my arms to them and order, "Have at me! I've missed you guys!"

T is the first to arrive. "You have not. If you missed me, you'd call once in a while."

"Forgive me," I tell her while grabbing her in a hug. "It's not every day a girl falls in love with a sexy Englishman."

"NO!" she yells in my ear, practically breaking my eardrum.

"Yes!" I squeeze her tightly with excitement. "We told each other this morning."

Jen sighs so loudly T and I both stop to stare at her. "Are you okay?" I ask.

"No. I'm broke, my parents hate me, my rent is due, and Brutus pooped on my foot this morning." I take a whiff and sure enough there's a little something extra coming from her direction. "AND, nobody loves me!"

"We love you," I tell her.

"I want big, sexy Englishman love!" she pouts.

"Girl, don't we all," T tells her. "Just wait until you meet this guy." She rolls her head back on her shoulders like she's stroking out on me.

I pull up a chair next to them. "I don't have enough business yet to hire you guys on full-time, but I'm hoping in a few months I will. Then I can help you get ahead a little," I say, looking at Jen.

"I don't have a few months," she says. "I stopped by St. Patrick's the other day and lit a candle, then I went out to a Jamaican neighborhood in Queens to buy a voodoo wealth charm. I even started stalking Liam Hemsworth because he was photographed at an art opening in SoHo and I can SO see him owning my stuff."

Jen's good people, but she's what you might call eccentric. "Do you know where he lives?" I ask.

"Not a clue."

"Girl, then how can you stalk him?" Teisha demands.

"I pretend he asked me to meet him at the gallery and then I wait while the owner calls him."

"Honey, that's creepy," T tells her.

"I know it is and yet I'm so desperate for help I've taken to lighting candles from a religion I don't even practice and I've started flirting with the black arts. Voodoo," she reminds us. "I need the universe to open up and provide already. Like, yesterday."

After inhaling my scone and starting another at a more relaxed pace, I say, "Maybe you need to pray or something."

"That's what the candle was all about," she tells me. "What I need to do is open my third eye and tap into the oneness of the universe. Only then will I be able to channel cosmic abundance." T gives me the side eye like she's wondering after Jen's mental health.

"We need to set up a proper girls' night," I tell them. "But unfortunately, right now I have to head back over to the East Side to have my tooth fixed." I stand up and grab the rest of my scone off the plate. "I'll call you both, I promise."

"Watch me not holding my breath," T says.

"T, I promise."

She rolls her eyes and gives me another hug. "Terrance moves out on me and now you too? Thank god Kwan hasn't abandoned me."

"What's that supposed to mean?" I ask. "Have you started dating Kwan?"

"I would never break the sacred bond between me and my toenail bedazzler by crossing the line and letting things get too personal." She pushes me toward the door and dramatically says, "Go! Leave me! Don't worry about me all alone up in Harlem!"

I giggle at her theatrics before hurrying out of the bakery. I decide I'll get across town quicker if I walk through the park. In addition, I'll also get to appreciate another stellar day in beautiful New York City. I'm so high on life right now, nothing can bring me down.

I walk into Dr. Pearlman's office with a smile on my face and greet the receptionist like she's my long-lost sister. She looks a little unnerved by my enthusiastic acknowledgment, but I don't care. I'm full of joy. I have carped my diem again and again in the last few weeks and I'm floating on cloud nine!

Dr. Pearlman comes in after Busty Boober—that's what I've nicknamed his assistant—straps a bib on me and makes me rinse with something that tastes like a cross between mouth wash and dirty dishwater. "Ms. Tompkins," he greets. "We've received a beautiful new tooth for you." He's got one of those tiny flashlights strapped to his head as he walks over to the counter and picks up a clear plastic baggie with my new front tooth in it.

After handing it to Busty, he picks up a pair of pliers and announces, "I'm just going to remove the temporary." He starts gently enough, but that ends pretty quickly when the temp doesn't budge.

After a particularly vicious yank, I scream, "Holy mother of God, OUCH!" Then I pull back and pinch my lips together so tightly he'll need a crowbar to open my mouth.

"I guess we better give you some Lidocaine." What was he waiting for? Is he some kind of sadist?

He comes at me with a cotton swab. "This is a topical numbing agent, so the shot won't hurt as badly." He rubs it on the roof of my mouth.

"Where am I getting the shot?" I ask nervously.

"Right where I'm applying the topical," he answers.

"You're going to shoot me on the roof of my mouth?!" I suddenly feel woozy and the room starts to spin. I think I'm going to pass out.

Dr. Pearlman picks up my hand and slaps at it firmly, "Stay with me. You're going to be just fine. I'll give you plenty of numbing agent, so we only have to do one shot." He picks up a cartoon-sized syringe and comes at me with it. I try to remind myself how happy I am in my life right now and that nothing can bring me down. It's not working.

My terror must be written all over my face because Dr. P asks if I'd like a diazepam.

I'm about to say no but Busty gives me a knowing nod. "It'll take the edge off."

Well, I definitely need to take the edge off at the moment. I answer to the affirmative, suck back the pill with a shot of water, then the two of them leave me alone for a few minutes for the numbing agent and the pill to kick in.

When he comes back, Dr. Pearlman motions for his assistant to be on hand to hold me down if necessary and my bladder almost gives way. I'm pretty sure I feel exactly like an Old West cowboy about to have a bullet removed with only a swig of whiskey and a towel to bite down on. I'm about to climb out of the chair when a sense of calm overtakes me, and I grin at Busty. "This is nice. I'm going to come here more often."

I close my eyes and open my mouth on cue, and happily there's nothing more than a mild burning sensation before the entire roof of my mouth and upper lip go completely numb. It takes no time after that for Dr. Pearlman to get the temp out and cement my new crown into place. "No eating hard or sticky food for twelve hours," he tells me. "You need to let the glue set well first."

After he leaves, Busty has me rinse my mouth out one more time before taking my bib from me. "Dr. Pearlman likes to follow-up with crowns on the front teeth, so please see the receptionist on your way out to set up another appointment."

I nod my head dumbly and stagger out of the room like a convict seeing daylight for the first time in ten years. Somehow the lights of the reception area are too bright and instead of feeling nice and relaxed, I feel … restless. I stop at the front desk and wait while the receptionist talks on the phone. I watch her, growing increasingly agitated by the second. Just then Busty comes out and says, "You forgot your purse."

I take it from her, saying, "Thanks, Busty."

Her head snaps back and she says, "What did you just call me?"

If I weren't stoned right now, I'd be super embarrassed. "Did I say that out loud?"

"Yeah, you did," she snaps.

I narrow my eyes at her, ready to fight even though I have no idea why. "You're the one without enough shirt on, not me!"

I clamp my hands over my mouth and gasp. "Sorry! I don't know what's wrong with me. I'm really angry right now."

Busty's face falls. "Oh, you might be having a reaction to the diazepam. Most people feel really chilled out on it, but some people have a bad reaction after a while, and they get super aggressive. I'd suggest going straight home."

Bad reaction? Go home? What?! I give her two very aggressive thumbs up and say, "Okay, will do."

The receptionist, who is still yakking away, pulls something out of the printer and snaps her fingers to get my attention. Well, that's rude. Maybe I should fight her. I pick up the piece of paper and see that it's a bill for my tooth. What's this all about? I thought Dr. Pearlman was fixing my tooth as a favor to Byron. I motion to the receptionist. After she puts her call on hold, I ask, "Am I supposed to pay this?"

She takes it from me and looks at it, then in a red pen, she circles a name in the upper left corner. "Noel Fitzwilliam has already paid. This is just a copy for your records."

"Noel Fitzwilliam paid?" I ask in shock. "I thought Dr. Pearlman was doing this as a favor for Byron Scott."

She looks confused. "I don't know who that is. But Mr. Fitzwilliam called in and pre-paid a few weeks ago. I remember because it's so unusual."

I grab the receipt and blindly turn around to leave while I try to make heads or tails out of what she said. Nope. I can't. In a daze, I walk to the nearest subway stop and take the next train down to Wall Street. I'm going to make Byron look me in the eye and tell me what's going on.

My face must look deformed from all the Lidocaine because I'm getting some strange looks from other passengers on the train. One lady even reaches into her purse and hands me a tissue. She offers it to me, saying, "Honey, you're drooling."

There's a faraway voice in my head telling me not to go into Fitzwilliam today. Not while I'm having a reaction to the drugs Dr. P gave me. I vaguely recall something about a big presentation but now I'm not sure if it's happening now or if it's over. But even if it is happening, Byron won't be in there so I can still yell at him.

By the time I get up to the forty-second floor, my upper lip feels huge and I've lost feeling in part of my tongue. How much Lidocaine did Dr. Pearlman give me? Byron sees me coming and his eyes bug out like I'm a circus freak.

"Sweetie, are you okay?"

I tip my head back and forth. "Denitht appointment." Then anger builds in my chest as I start at him. "Byron, I think there's thomething you need to tell me." I sound stern like a schoolteacher who just caught someone putting a wad of chewed gum under their desk.

He's trying so hard to look innocent, he looks guilty. I push it. "I know all about it, Byron. Feth up and I might forgive you thomeday."

He folds like a house of cards in a tornado. "I'm so sorry! I didn't know he was pretending to be me until you'd been texting him for ages!"

What is he talking about?

He continues, "It's just that Noel really liked you and really wanted to get to know you, so he pretended to be me so he could do that."

What?!

Byron keeps going. "But it's not as creepy as it sounds, I promise. Noel and I have pretended to be each other ever since we were little boys." He must note the horror in my eyes, because he hurries to say, "It's a very common thing for twins to do."

"Your hith bruther?!" I scream.

"Oh dear, he didn't tell you? I thought he would have mentioned that by now."

My entire body feels as numb as my mouth as I try to process what I've just heard. Mortification floods my extremities as I remember telling Byron how hot I was for his boss. And all the time I was saying that to Noel. OMG. "No and he didn't tell me that I wath texthting him and not you … and neither did you. The lieth! The lieth you two have told!"

"Oh my god, sweetie, I'm so sorry," Byron says, trying to hug me.

I shake him off. "You're a liar. And tho ith Noel."

"Does it make a difference that we did it because he liked you so much?"

I glare at him until he says, "I suppose not." Then a slightly confused look crosses his face. "Wait. If you weren't talking about the texting or our being brothers, what were you talking about?"

I hand him the receipt from Dr. Pearlman's office. "Thith."

He looks at it and says, "Oh. That."

Rage fills my brain and I demand, "Where ith he?"

"He's presenting to the Walters in the conference room."

I spin on my heel and stalk down the hall, readying myself for battle.

"You can't go in there, Aimée," he says as I storm by.

"Really?" I turn around and yell. "Whoth gonna thtop me?!"

Chapter Thirty-Four

Noel

"And here, you'll note we've found a way to provide the illusion of an invisible rainwater collection system by creating a false front that matches the surrounding materials." Pausing for a second, I glance back at the slide on the wall behind me. One click of the remote adds another layer to the image, and instantly, the pipes disappear. I look over at Walter Junior, and see he's nodding, which I take as a very good sign.

A thump on the glass wall near the door causes everyone to turn. And there's the love of my life, drooling and glaring at me while she holds a piece of paper against the glass. I lean forward and narrow my eyes, but from my current vantage point, I have no idea what it is. I give her a "not now" look, but she doesn't budge like I hoped she would.

"What is the caterer doing here?" Cindy asks loudly. "Does she really need to be paid right this very second? Pushy, much?"

"There must be a serious problem," I say in a sharp tone. Turning to the Walters, I add, "I'm very sorry. I'll just need a minute." Then, looking at Ali, I ask him to take over.

As soon as I'm out in the hall, I head straight for my office so as to avoid curious onlookers while I find out what's going on. "I don't know what could possibly be so pressing that you had to interrupt the most important presentation of my life," I tell Aimée.

She follows me, waving the paper near my shoulder. "Thith!"

I snatch it from her and read it, then stop. "Oh, this." Shit. Bollocks. Double damn. Bugger. "I can explain."

Folding her arms across her chest, she raises her voice, her nostrils in full-flare mode. "Oh, really? Can you explain how you and Byron are acthually twinth and you're not just hith bosth? And that the whole time I was texthing him I wath really texthing you???!!!" She unfolds her arms and pokes me on the upper chest for good measure.

"Aimée … I was going to tell you—"

"When? After we got married and had a couple of kidth? Or maybe when you were on your death bed?" she yells.

"Please lower your voice," I say, wishing we'd made it all the way back to my office and we weren't having this conversation in the hallway.

"Why? Am I embarrathing you?! I wouldn't want to humiliate you. God knowth it's no fun to be humiliated!"

"Aimée, please, I know what I did was wrong and I promise I'll never do anything like this again," I say, placing both hands carefully on her upper arms. "But, can we just discuss this at home in private?

There's so much I need to explain and I can't have this conversation right at this moment."

"It'th now or never," she says, shrugging away from me. "Becauth you're not going to see me at your home again." She nods once and adds, "I'm getting my stuff right now. I'll be gone before you get back!"

"Please, let's not—"

Pointing one finger in my face, she barks out, "I am not overreacting!"

"I wasn't going to say that." *I was totally going to say that.*

Over her shoulder, Cindy snaps her fingers. "Umm, Noel? Ali's done and if you don't get back in there, I'm pretty sure they're going to leave."

I look at Cindy, and I say, "Yes, of course. Straight away."

I turn back to Aimée, but she's already moved past me and is storming down the hall. Son of a bitch. Following her, I add, "Aimée, please, just wait in my office, okay? I promise I can make it right." I don't know if that's true, but I am willing to spend the rest of my life trying.

She flips me the middle finger over her shoulder and says, "Make thith right!"

When she passes Byron, she yells, "That goath for you too!"

With that, she swings the glass door open so hard, it bounces back and hits her on the shoulder as she walks out, bumping her into the other glass door. She makes a heartbreaking yipping sound like a small dog who just had one foot stepped on, but she doesn't break her stride. A few seconds later, the elevator

247

doors open, and she disappears, but not before giving my brother and me double middle fingers. One for each of us, I suppose.

Byron looks at me. "So, you still hadn't told her, then? I really thought you would have by now."

"Oh, sod off," I say, turning around and heading back to a room full of my staff and my most important clients, who all now think I allow the caterer to boss me around. *Very confidence-inspiring, Noel. Just brilliant. Way to cock up your entire life all in one afternoon.*

Chapter Thirty-Five

Aimée

I send Teisha an SOS.

AiméeT: I just broke up with Noel. You know how I started texting Byron after our first gig at F&A? Turns out I wasn't. I was texting Noel the whole time!

T: ...

AiméeT: And you know how Byron is Noel's assistant? Well, he's also his twin brother!

T: ...

AiméeT: I have been duped! I've been treated like a toy, a floozy, a non-equal, and I'm not going to stand for it!

T: ...

AiméeT: Are you listening to me?!

T: SLOW down! Yes, I'm listening, but I'm also trying to absorb this. You're saying the whole time you were complaining to Byron about Noel, you were really complaining to Noel?

AiméeT: YES!

T: Oh sweetie, are you coming home?

AiméeT: Yes.

T: Okay, I'll see you there in about an hour when I'm off. Hang tough, sister, we got this.

AiméeT: -sad face-crying face-broken heart-broken heart-broken heart-

As soon as I exit the subway on Noel's block, my anger morphs to sadness at warp speed. Why did this have to happen to me? I love Noel. Retraction. I loved Noel. He was everything I could have ever wanted in a boyfriend and more. I just didn't count on him being a low down dirty rotten scum-sucking liar.

Once I get up to the apartment, I make quick work of packing up the stuff I have there. Part of me wants to trash the place as a sign of my broken heart. You know, break stuff—I'm eyeing you, Limoges coffee service—throw all the food in the fridge into the garbage, really blow through this place like a tornado.

Ultimately, I decide that would be crossing the line of my own self-respect, so I simply pull the roses he gave me out of their vase and toss them in the garbage. Leaving the lid up, of course. While I believe in maintaining dignity, I'm also a real fan of passive-aggressive statements.

Heaving my overnight bag over my shoulder, I take one last look at Noel's super gorgeous apartment and try to memorize everything. While I'm devastated beyond belief, I never want to forget these last beautiful weeks before my heart was dashed upon the rocky shore of love. I'm no poet, but at the moment I feel positively Byronic.

By the time I get back up to Harlem, my mouth is no longer numb, which means I can speak normally but also, my mouth is really sore, which just adds insult to injury. T is already home and has laid out the break-up buffet—marshmallow fluff, chocolate syrup, a can of spray whipping cream, and a jar of Spanish olives. *You don't eat them all together. It more like a spoonful of this, a squirt of that, a spray of this and a salty topper.*

I drop my bag and let her throw her arms around me. "I think we need to reread all the texts to make sure this is as bad as you think it is," she says after a minute.

"It's bad, T. So, so bad," I say, cringing. "And the lies? It's unforgivable. Maybe if he'd told me three weeks ago when things started for real, I might have been able to forgive him. But he kept this to himself for too long to believe he was ever going to confess. And he pulled Byron into his deception! I've lost my beautiful British boyfriend and we've both lost our new gay best friend!" I'm full-on wailing now.

"Damn," T says while spraying the whipped cream directly into her mouth. After she swallows it, she says, "Hand me your phone."

We spend the next two hours going through every single text Noel and I shared while he pretended to be his brother. Lowlights include "For a gig like that, I'll kiss his feet and call him daddy," and me moaning about how he turned me down after our "business dinner." The things I said to him are so embarrassing I might just have to give up texting altogether. After all, you never really know who's on the other side, do you?

At five o'clock, the street buzzer goes off, alerting us that someone wants to come up. Looking out the window, I tell Teisha, "Don't answer it. It's Noel."

She goes straight to the refrigerator and grabs a dozen eggs and brings them to me. I open the window and yell down six floors, "Go home, Noel! I don't want to talk to you ever again!"

He looks up and spots me. "Aimée, please! I know I messed up. I do. But I promise you I'll never do anything like that again. Only the truth from here on out."

"Once a liar, always a liar," I reply.

"I love you, Aimée, in a way I've never loved anyone before and never will again. You're it for me and yes, I was a total git to do what I did. And the entire time, I knew I had to stop, but I just couldn't because it would have meant I wouldn't have had any contact with you. I've never in my life done anything even close to as stupid or dishonest and I would never do something like it again." Dozens of people have stopped walking and are now watching, which must be super-humiliating for him. It kind of makes me happy, to be honest.

He looks so pathetic down there in his rumpled suit. I briefly wonder how the rest of his presentation went, but there is no way in hell I'd ever ask him. That's not any of my business now that he's not my boyfriend, or client probably. Damn, that's going to be a double sting.

"Please, will you just let me up so we can talk? Or come down? Either's good. I just don't want things to end this way." He runs his hand through his hair, leaving it sticking up just like it does after you-know-what. "Or at all, really. I meant everything I said to you, even when I was pretending to be Byron."

A woman walks past him, giving him the side-eye, then looks up at me and yells, "Shut the window, honey, and forget him!"

T looks at me. "You're too quiet. You're not actually considering taking him back, are you?"

"Pfft, no!" I say, even though that's exactly what I was just thinking. Just for a milli-second. She picks up her phone and makes a call. I hear her say, "Kwan, we've got a rat at the front door. Would you mind chasing it away for us?"

Moments later, Kwan storms out of The Finger and stalks across street looking like he's ready to kick some serious butt. When he spots Noel, he looks skyward and calls T back. She picks up and affirms, "That's him."

When he's about five feet from Noel, Kwan pulls a nail file out of his pocket and starts switching it from hand to hand like he's a member of the Jets in *West Side Story*. All that's missing is some whistling and singing.

I watch as Noel holds his hands up and says, "Can I help you?"

Kwan leans forward and says, "Leave my friends alone."

"And who are you exactly?" Noel asks.

"I their nail man," he says, pointing up to us with the nail file.

Noel looks up at me. "I'll go if this is really what you want, Aimée. But you have to know I love you and nothing will ever change that."

With that, he walks away, stuffing his hands in his pants pockets, looking thoroughly dejected. As he should. Kwan give us a thumbs up, then turns and walks away.

I turn to Teisha. "Kwan is something of a man of mystery, isn't he?"

She nods. "He is a good friend with some special skills, that's for sure. Not every man has a knack for filing calluses and can also double as a bodyguard."

"You should go out with him sometime, T," I tell my friend. It hasn't passed my notice how her eyes glaze over fondly when she talks about him.

"Maybe," she says noncommittally. "But first, let's run you a hot bath. While you have a therapeutic soak, I'll call for Chinese and queue up *Love Actually*. A little MSG and a good cry can fix anything."

Once upon a time, I might have agreed with her. Right now, I'm not so sure.

Chapter Thirty-Six

Noel
Three Weeks Later

One of the great ironies of life is that you can be perfectly fine all by yourself for many years—happy even. But then you meet the one, totally cock it up, and when you try to go back to your old life, it feels like an itchy jumper that's three sizes too small. And for some ungodly reason, it's nearly super-glued on so you can't take off.

On the surface, my life looks like everything is coming up roses. Brown, Brown, and Green officially announced our partnership as the architects of One Rosenthal. I had been worried that Walter Junior would perhaps take issue with what had happened at Bull Market, but it turns out, he ended up picking up some rando and totally forgot about Aimée. Also, he thinks we're good buddies somehow and keeps hinting that we should play squash again soon. Not bloody likely.

We're in full swing on the project, our team is busy finalizing everything so we can go over it with the construction crew. It's enough work to keep us hopping for years and it's going to be the greatest achievement of my career—it's what I've been building toward since I first picked up a mechanical pencil all those years ago and drew up a treehouse for an assignment at uni. I should be beyond thrilled. Celebrating, ecstatic. The congratulatory phone calls have been coming in by the dozen, and yet … I don't give a dead rat's arse because I've ruined the one thing that actually makes life worth living—the relationship with the woman I love.

If I could go back and do it all differently, I would. Right from the moment she skidded into my arms. Well, maybe not that bit, but the rest, absolutely. I wouldn't have been a coward. I would have played it straight with her and told her the truth about everything from day one—who Byron really is to me, how I feel about her, my fears about disappointing her—everything. And right now, I'd be back at my apartment tapping away on my laptop and sneaking glances at her while she invents another amazing dish. I'd be planning a romantic getaway for us, thinking about whisking her home to London to meet my family and friends. I know it sounds crazy-fast, but it wouldn't be too much longer before I would have been picking out a ring.

Those thoughts haunt me every hour of every day, and I honestly don't know when (or if) they'll ever stop. The worst has been the waiting, the praying she'll show up for the employee appreciation lunch, but she sends Teisha in her place. I don't blame her, but the level of disappointment when the elevator door opens and she's not there has been a real kick in the gut. In spite of myself, I get my hopes up only to have them crushed with the force of a wrecking ball when I see it's not her. Teisha hates me, by the way, as any good best friend would, I suppose. She glares at me while she slaps my food on a plate, and I swear, she mutters the word "liar" as soon as I turn my back. Which I am.

I grab my empty coffee mug and make my way toward the kitchen. I'm pretty much surviving on caffeine since I find I can no longer sleep without Aimée in my arms. When I pass Byron's desk, he says, "You're not going to try to talk to Teisha again, are you?"

"No," I say, rolling my eyes, even though that's exactly what I'm going to do.

"Good, because she's serving deviled eggs, which are perfect for sling-shotting off a spoon," he says while he scrolls on his mobile. "I think you may have to let it lie, Noel. Aimée's made it more than clear she's done with both of us. Shame, really, because I miss her."

"Oh, do you?" I ask. "How awful for you."

Rolling his eyes, he says, "I know it's not easy for you either. Don't think it escaped my notice that you're sleeping here every night, and call it twin-tuition, but I know it's because your place feels too empty without her."

I don't answer because I can't bear to admit the sad truth.

"Um-hmm, thought so."

When I get to the kitchen, Teisha's there, humming while she lights the propane burner under one of the serving trays. I offer her a weary smile and get the usual stink-eye in return. "Hi, Teisha."

She grunts in response while I walk past her to the coffee maker. I fill up my mug, then turn to her. "Is she okay?"

"That is none of your beeswax," she answers without making eye-contact.

"You're right, but I just … have to know that she'll be okay," I say with a sigh.

"She'll be just fine, no thanks to you."

Damn it. "So, she's *not* okay."

"I didn't say that." Teisha looks up at me for a second. "But she will be when she finds someone worthy of her, which should happen tomorrow night because I'm taking her dancing. Rebound, Mr. Right—doesn't matter so long as he's not a lying scumbag."

"Teisha, if I could go back—"

She holds up one hand. "Save it. And you can stop sending flowers and all those fancy meals over. They just end up in the trash." She pauses for a second, then adds, "Well, not the food. We eat it and it's pretty darn good so you can keep ordering dinners for us. But it's not going to change her mind and you need to know that."

"Is there anything I can do to get her back?" I ask, sounding every bit as pathetic as I feel. "I'd literally do anything."

"Can you design a time machine and go back and not be a total douche canoe?" she asks, planting one hand on her hip.

"If I could, believe me, I'd drop everything and start working on it."

She stares at me for a minute, then says, "You look like a steaming pile of crap."

Nodding, I say, "I feel like it. I haven't been sleeping."

Her face softens. "So, you really are broken up over Aimée. I thought you'd have moved on by now."

"I don't think I can. She was it for me," I say, forcing myself to lay my soul bare to this woman who clearly can't stand me. "I've never adored someone the way I do her. Not even close. I'm a pathetic mess. I lie awake all night thinking of the things I should have done differently, and there are just so many of them. I know it's too late to fix it. I was beyond stupid."

"Yeah, you were," Teisha offers.

Cindy pokes her head in the door and says, "Noel, Jack and I need to see you."

I nod, then push off the counter and start for the hall. "Listen, Teisha, if there's ever anything she needs, I'll be there for her. Anything at all. I just want her to be happy, even if I can't be part of that."

Chapter Thirty-Seven

Aimée

"Well, shit," I hear Teisha mutter as she walks into the apartment while stuffing her phone into her pocket.

"Bad news?" I ask, immediately wondering what happened at the Fitzwilliam lunch today.

"Nah, everything's okay. Listen"—she drops her purse and kicks off her shoes before joining me in the living room—"Noel is really sorry. Like really, really sorry."

"Are you suggesting I take him back? After what he did to me?" I can't believe she's saying that. I forget all about the invoice I was itemizing and shut my laptop, inwardly preparing myself for a big, BIG argument.

"I'm saying that the two of you owe it to each other to meet up and talk. That's all. If it's nothing more than closure, then fine. But having just seen him, I can tell you that man is not getting over you. Maybe ever."

I snort and roll my eyes. "Pu-lease. Deception is his thing, T. Whatever he told you is a *lie*."

"It wasn't so much what he said, but how he looked—like he hasn't slept in weeks. Maybe he drew on big dark circles under his eyes, but I highly doubt it," she says. "Plus, Byron told me he's been sleeping at his office since you left because he can't stand to go home. It's too lonely for him now."

I throw my head back in evil laughter. "Come *on*! You can't take Byron's word for it. He's his brother's little puppet. He'll say whatever Noel orders him to."

Shrugging, T says, "For what it's worth, I believe him."

Biting my lip, I can't help but consider her words. Nope. Just no. "Seriously, T, you cannot take his side in this."

"I'm not, but as your bestie, I think you deserve to know that I'm not entirely sure you're making the right decision here. You were really frigging happy with Noel. That's a fact. And other than him messing things up before you started dating, he treated you like gold. He was the perfect boyfriend."

"Do me a favor and don't remind me. This is hard enough as it is without you second-guessing me!" I raise my voice, feeling tears prick my eyes. "It's over. We're through, so just leave it alone already."

She folds her arms across her chest. "If it's really over, then act like it because all this moping around the apartment you've been doing is driving me insane."

"You said you understood," I accuse while my chin sinks down toward my breastbone and my hands

261

ball up into fists. It's not like I'm going to punch my best friend, it just that when I feel like I'm being attacked, I curl up like a turtle retreating into its shell.

"I do understand! I understand so much I'm feeling your pain right along with you. It's just that, Aimes, you've reached the point of this thing where you're prolonging your anguish. If he's really such a horrible person, you should be glad to be free of him. You should be throwing yourself a big party, not lying in the fetal position watching *Titanic* on repeat. You gotta shake it off."

"I'm going dancing with you tomorrow night, what more do you want?" I stand up and march toward my bedroom door.

Before I get there, she answers, "I want you to quit giving away your power. You are letting Noel make you sad when you should be out having fun and enjoying the fact that you're no longer stuck working for someone else for tips. Your business is taking off in a serious way. But instead of savoring this moment, you're crying in your tea over a man. You need to snap out of it and start acting like the strong woman you claim to be. Either that, or dig deep and find forgiveness in your heart. The man still loves you."

"Did he say that?" I turn around and walk toward her. Shaking my head, I say, "No. Don't tell me."

"He did say that—and so much more," Teisha yells, waving a finger at me. "But here's the thing. I'm not going to tell you what he said because *he* should be telling you, and you should be letting him.

So, you have two choices, buck up already, or have the courage to put this thing to bed the right way."

I'm so mad right now I could spit nails. The girlfriend code clearly states that the person who has had the breakup is the one who gets to decide how best to mourn that breakup. I'm not even a month into this. And yes, while I know we were only together for three weeks, they were three perfect weeks. They were bliss. Actually, better than bliss, they were euphoric. He really was the perfect boyfriend—attentive, fun, sweet, thoughtful, respectful. He cheered for me on my good days and rubbed my shoulders when I was tired. That's why I'm not bouncing back. You can't fall out of love quicker than you fall into it. If anything, it's harder to fall out of love because you have all of those beautiful memories of when life was wonderful. You know what you're missing.

"I'm going for a walk," I tell T before grabbing my jean jacket and heading to the door.

"Good. You need to blow some of the stink off you, girl. Feel the sunshine on your face ... embrace your inner ..." Slam!

I don't know where I'm going right now, but I need to get away. I don't need anyone telling me how to handle my pain, certainly not someone who isn't woman enough to go after the guy she's been making eyes at forever. She'll let a man scrub her feet and groom her nails, but she won't do anything else. The hypocrisy! Telling me how to live my life when she's the mayor of Avoidance Land. That's it. I'm going to The Finger to talk to Kwan.

I stride down the street with such purpose I almost knock over a man I'm guessing is either a professional prize fighter or a hitman for the mob. "Chill, sister," he tells me. "Slow it down."

I stop walking and turn on him with enough mad that I'm pretty sure I could take him in two rounds. He rightly looks alarmed and hurries away. Do not mess with me, people! I am not in the mood!

As I walk into The Finger, Kwan calls out, "Hello, Aimée, friend of queen." He doesn't really think T is named Queen Latifah, does he?

"Hey, Kwan. Do you have time to give me a pedicure?"

He points to an empty massage chair. "Take a seat."

I roll up my pant legs and put my feet in the tub while the hot soapy water pours in around me. As soon as Kwan sits down, I ask, "What's the deal with you and Teisha?"

"Queen is my best customer." He starts to take my nail polish off without offering anything else.

"She's been coming in here for what, two or three years?" I ask.

"Two-years and eight months." He starts to file my hoofs down with a righteous pumice stone. I sit back and let him.

Once he rinses and dries my feet and starts to massage my legs, I ask, "Why haven't you ever asked Teisha out on a date?"

He looks up at me from the top of his eyes and says, "She would not go out with me."

"How do you know if you don't ask her?" I practically yell.

"She is a beautiful woman." He stops massaging and pantomimes, "Tall, nice body. She could do better than a man who gives pedicures for a living."

"You don't know what you're talking about, Kwan. You must realize that no woman needs as many pedicures as Teisha gets. She comes in here because she's hoping something might happen." In my mind I'm thinking, *how do you like that, T? I can interfere in your love life, too!*

He goes back to my massage.

"But you want to go out with her, yes?"

He slowly nods his head but doesn't make eye contact.

"Okay," I tell him. "Teisha and I are going dancing tomorrow night. I think you should show up at the club and ask her to dance." I pull out my purse and write down the name and address of where we're going. "Meet us there at ten o'clock tomorrow night."

Kwan takes the paper and slips it into his pocket without indicating one way or the other if he's going to show. He finishes the rest of my pedicure in near-silence, which actually works for me because I want to go back to stewing about what T said to me about lacking the courage to face Noel. Even though I secretly think she might be right, I will never admit to it.

I don't see Teisha for the rest of the afternoon. I think she beat it out of the apartment because she doesn't want another scene. And believe me, after talking to Kwan and getting the same vibe off him that she gives—pathetic fawning with a side of unrequited love—I could give her a scene to end all scenes.

I don't know what time she comes home, but she's gone for work before I wake up the next day. My sleep cycle is totally screwy since Noel and I broke up. I lie awake all night thinking about him, wishing that he had been straight with me. I don't actually fall asleep until the muscles in my eyelids can't take it anymore and finally give in.

I wake up at two when my phone pings with a text from my bossy, bossy friend.

> T: Be ready to leave at nine tonight. I don't care if you're still mad at me, we're going dancing!

Oh, she's got that right. We are definitely going dancing and she's going to face the music with Kwan, once and for all.

Teisha doesn't come home until seven. I don't ask where she's been all day. In fact, the first thing I say to her is, "Wear your purple dress," and that's twenty minutes before we leave.

"What's wrong with this dress?" she snaps at me while staring down at her red slip dress.

"You look like royalty in the purple one. You should look like a queen tonight." My tone is significantly softer when I say that.

T comes over to me and wraps me in her arms. "Tough love is still love," she tells me.

I hug her back, glad that we're not fighting any more. "Remember you said that," I counter, before pulling back and finishing putting on my earrings.

We head out the door to HaDa moments later and at long last, the air between us is finally light again.

The club is loud and crowded. There are flashing lights and a steady bass is booming through the ether like a heartbeat. I couldn't describe the décor of this place if my life depended on it, but the feeling is one of pure freedom. I pull T out to the dance floor and close my eyes as the rhythmic pulse flows through me.

I'm dancing and twirling and spinning. I'm no longer me, I'm an extension of the music. At some point, I lose T and when I search the dance floor, I spot her dirty dancing with Kwan. I give them the double thumbs up and get back into my own groove. I feel like I'm finally exorcizing some demons and I don't want to stop until I know I've succeeded. After I leave the dance floor, I turn around and try to locate Teisha. That's when I see him. Not the *him* that I love—that's right, I haven't fallen out of love with Noel yet. I lock eyes with his twin brother.

Byron waves to me from a table near the bar. I'm at a crossroads, do I suck it up and let him apologize— his transgressions *were* smaller than Noel's after all—or do I walk away and pretend he doesn't exist either?

When I approach him, he stands and opens his arms to me.

"Are you stalking me?" I demand, ignoring his obvious bid for a hug.

"I told *you* about this place." He sits back down, indicating that I should join him.

I do. "What are you doing here?" I want to know.

"I was supposed to meet my boyfriend, but he canceled." I'm not sure I believe him. He continues, "Aimée Tompkins, you temperamental little minx, I miss you. I know you're furious with Noel, but I have never lied to you."

"Lies of omission are still lies, Byron." I pull his drink over and take a large sip out of it.

He nods his head. "Be that as it may, I miss my fruit fly and I want her back."

"How can I be friends with the man whose brother broke my heart?" I demand.

"One day at a time, darling. I promise to never mention Noel, as long as you promise to do the same."

My heart has known too much loss in the last few weeks. I'm vulnerable and sad, and I really do need my Byron fix.

"Okay," I tell him. Then I throw my arms around him as a tear falls onto his shoulder.

Chapter Thirty-Eight

Noel

"I cannot believe I'm doing this," I say as soon as Byron gets into the town car. We're heading out to dinner at Celeste, a notoriously romantic restaurant, with Byron's jazz musician, Jay, and Jay's ex, Cole (also a jazz musician), who's in town for a gig.

"Good lord, man, quit grumbling already." Byron slams his knee into mine to push me farther into the cavern of the car's backseat.

"You're certain this Cole knows I'm not gay? I wouldn't want him to think this is a blind date, and you know, tease him with all this," I say, gesturing to my body. I've been trying to force a sense of humor back into my life the last couple of days, but it's been painful.

"He knows! I told you that eighty times already." Byron huffs, settling next me.

"I just don't see why you needed a fourth for dinner," I say again.

"Because Cole is notorious for making Jay feel terrible about himself, so we thought having you there will ensure he's on his best behavior. Also, you're much better at comebacks than I am. I'm counting on you to verbally slay Cole if he starts criticizing Jay, especially his thighs. If that bastard mentions Jay's thighs, you jump in."

I close my eyes and rub the bridge of my nose. "Why would Jay even want to see someone like that?"

"It's a revenge dinner," Byron scoffs. "Jay's going to show me off so Cole knows Jay's over him and that he can do much better."

"This is a terrible way to spend a Tuesday night," I mutter, glancing out at a guy on the sidewalk selling watches out of a briefcase. He looks about as dodgy as this evening feels. "I never should have said yes."

"Well, it's too late to back out now. Plus, it's getting you out of your pathetic office/rooming house for a few hours," Byron says, reaching over and picking some lint off my suit jacket. "Also, you owe me after everything I do for you."

"Like what exactly?" Spilling the beans to my girlfriend and ruining my life? I don't say that though. I do have enough self-awareness to realize I brought that whole situation on myself.

"What do I do for you?" Byron makes a list on his fingers. "Filing, fetching coffee, sending emails…"

"That's called a job, and you get paid rather well for it," I quip.

He digs his pointer finger into my shoulder. "That snotty comeback is why I need you," he says with a smile. "Keep practicing so you'll be in top form for dinner."

Rolling my eyes, I sigh. "Fine."

"Buck up, little camper," Byron says. "It's springtime in New York. Love is in the air."

"Not for me," I murmur, my chest aching at the very thought of love. Not to mention my shoulder from Byron's rather aggressive jabbing.

"Well, who knows? Maybe tonight will be the beginning of something new for you?"

"With Cole, the trombonist?" I'm not quite that far gone that I've given up the thought of women entirely.

When we get to the restaurant, we find the expansive lobby packed with clusters of people waiting for tables. Byron tells me to wait while he hurries over to the maître d' to announce our arrival. He waves to me, and when I join them, we start winding our way through the dimly lit dining room.

By the looks of our fellow diners, I'm assuming they're on first dates or celebrating anniversaries—very lovey-dovey goings on. I pull my mobile out of my pocket and flick through my notifications while we walk, hoping to avoid the sight of happy people.

When we arrive at our table, I hear, "Oh, hell, no!"

I glance up and my stomach drops to my knees. Aimée is sitting at the table with Teisha. She looks breathtakingly beautiful in her navy dress, with her hair swept up off her neck. Boy, does she look furious. I stare with my jaw hanging down like an idiot as I try to sort out what's happening. She seems to be much quicker figuring this out than I am, because she's already getting up, giving Teisha a good tongue-lashing.

When she looks up at me, she says, "I suppose you orchestrated this."

"I'm as shocked as you are," I manage.

Teisha stands, grabs Aimée by the shoulders, and sits her back down, while Byron pushes me into the chair across from her. Resting her hands on the table, Teisha leans down and announces, "Byron and I have had enough of you two with your sad sighs and all the curling up in a ball watching Leo and Kate."

"I've done no such thing," I say defensively. Okay, maybe once. Twice tops, but that was two weeks ago.

Byron plants his hands on his hips. "You're even worse. Tell Aimée why you haven't gone home since she dumped you! Tell her!"

Swallowing, I mutter, "I don't think she wants to hear it." I risk a glance at her, before saying, "I'm very sorry about this. I was told I was coming here as some sort of a wingman for my brother. I'll go. I know you don't ever want to see me again."

I start to get up, but am quickly stopped by Teisha who leans in and hisses, "Sit your sorry ass down or I'll start yelling and make a huge scene in front of all these people."

I stare up at her for a moment, trying to decide if I'm going to let myself be bossed around by my ex's best friend. I look at Aimée and ask, "She'll do it, won't she?"

Aimée nods reluctantly.

Teisha continues, "Byron and I will be at the bar, right over there, watching you." She points over her shoulder with her thumb. "Don't even think of leaving until you've had a proper meal. That includes dessert and after-dinner drinks."

Byron gives us a firm nod. "Get talking and straighten yourselves out already. The people who love you most are sick to death of you."

With that, they link arms and walk away, leaving us to our awkward silence.

"So, how have you been?" I ask, sounding utterly lame.

Aimée straightens her back. "Good. Great, really. Lots of business coming in. I'll be able to pay you in full for the tooth soon."

I'm about to tell her not to bother, but I know it's useless. She needs to do it. "I'm glad you're doing well. I hope for that every day."

"I saw the big announcement about One Rosenthal," she says stiffly. "Congratulations."

The waiter comes by with a basket of warm rolls and a bottle of sparkling water. He fills our glasses, then says, "I'm Wesley, I'll be your server this evening. Our sommelier will be by in a few moments to help you select some wine."

Aimée and I both thank him, and he disappears while I lift the basket and offer her a roll. She shakes her head, even though we both know she wants one. "No soft, warm buns for you?" I tease.

That almost earns me a grin. "No, thank you. I'm suddenly not all that hungry."

"I suppose not," I answer. "Listen, we don't have to let those two yahoos decide how we spend our evening. If sitting here with me repulses you, I'll keep them busy while you make a run for it."

"I don't find you repulsive," Aimée murmurs. After a brief pause, she adds, "Which is part of the problem. You're all …" She points up and down at me. "Gorgeous and charming with your posh accent and your tailored suit and your gentlemanly ways." She imitates me, "If sitting here with me repulses you, I'll keep them busy while you make a run for it."

"I can be rude if it'll help," I offer.

"It won't work if you're only doing it to make my life easier," she says, looking irritated.

"Righto, bad idea," I answer, scratching my head.

"Let's just order some food and eat so we can get the hell out of here. Teisha will never let it go if I don't go through with this."

"In that case, let the charade begin."

She opens the black menu in front of her and starts studying the choices. I study her. After a second, she clears her throat and whispers, "There aren't any prices on mine. Does yours have them?"

I shake my head. "I'm afraid not."

Her shoulders drop and she chews on her bottom lip for a second. "I'll just have some soup," she says, closing the menu.

"And I won't try to talk you into ordering a proper meal or offer to pay for it because I know that would bother you."

She lifts her chin and straightens her back. "Damn straight, it would. I'm already in deep to you for the dentist. I don't need to add a few hundred for dinner too."

A man in a tuxedo stops at our table and gives us a slick smile. "Good evening. I'm Peter, the master sommelier. If you already know what you're going to eat, I will select the perfect accompaniment to your meal."

Aimée smiles up at him. "No wine, thank you."

"No wine?" he asks, wrinkling his nose up.

"She's pregnant," I blurt out, while giving him a wink.

"I am not!" Ah, Aimée doesn't want to play.

"She gets very frisky when she drinks and she's currently mad at me." Before she can yell at me about that, I continue, "So, how about this Peter, I'll drink for two. Just bring me whatever wine you would choose for both of us and I promise to give it my best shot."

Peter nods his head once before marching away like he's about to go into battle. Aimée reaches into the breadbasket and throws a roll at me. "Don't be ridiculous. You are not going to sit here and drink for both of us."

"Am too," I tell her while breaking the roll in two and buttering half. "I might eat for two as well, if you refuse to order more than soup."

"All I want is soup," she maintains. "I hate to disappoint you, Noel, but it's not part of my job description to do whatever you tell me to. All I am to you is your caterer."

"My caterer who bloody well won't even show up at the job."

She shoots me one of those looks that's a cross between "you didn't just say that" and "I will make you pay in ways that will render you incapable of fathering children" but she doesn't actually say anything.

"How was that?" I ask. "Sufficiently rude enough for you to hate me?"

"Pretty good, actually," she says.

Sighing, I say, "Do you really hate me?" My gut turns to stone while I await her answer.

"I'm trying so hard to," she says, her eyes filled with hurt. "What you did was ..."

"Unforgivable, I know," I answer. "Totally unforgivable."

"It was. And as the weeks go on, I keep realizing the lengths you went to in order to keep up the ruse—you must have had to change your cell phone number when we actually started dating."

I nod and look down at the candle in the center of the table. "I would have done anything so that you never had to find out what a despicable snake I was."

"You basically stalked me, Noel," she adds quietly.

My chest aches. "It never felt like that to me. It felt like I was getting to know the loveliest, funniest woman in the world. It felt like all my birthday and Christmas gifts for the rest of my life wrapped into one. I didn't have the strength to resist you."

She counters, "If you wanted to go out with me, you should have just asked."

"I should have, yes." I sigh, then say, "At first, when you accidentally texted me instead of Byron, I thought it was amusing—you were writing about how much you hated me. I didn't think it would go far, and I fully intended to let you off the hook right then.

But then you wrote about how broke you were and I wanted to help you … and somehow, I couldn't bring myself to tell you the truth because I didn't want to stop having something that connected me to you. Anything, even if it was a lie."

Wesley the waiter comes back, and asks, "Have you decided?"

"I'll have the mushroom soup, please," Aimée says.

I look up at Wesley, "I'll have the filet and the lobster."

"Very good," he says. "Would you like any appetizers?" He's staring at me in something akin to awe at my ordering two entrees—the most expensive on the menu, no less. My menu does have the prices.

"Please," I tell him. "I'll have the braised sweetbreads and the crab cakes." Before he can walk away, I add, "And the Caesar salad for two."

"Yes, sir." He clicks his heels together in what I'm assuming is anticipation of a huge tip. With the size of our bill, he's going to make out right well for himself.

"I am not eating all that food with you," Aimée says determinedly. I love how tough she acts. But if I know her, and I do, she will not be able to resist trying the cuisine here.

"I absolutely won't allow it," I tease. "This is my food and if you want something other than a teaspoon full of bisque, you'll have to order it for yourself."

Aimée tries to stifle the smile coming to her face but is not totally successful.

"I'm sorry if my adorable sense of humor is making it hard to be mad at me. I'll cut that out."

Giving me a crooked smile, she says, "Please do."

I stare at her, trying to memorize every detail of her face in case this is the last time I'm graced with the sight of it. "What were we talking about?"

"How you justified lying to me for so long…"

"Right. That," I say, feeling my mouth go dry. "It was pathetic. The entire thing. And I have literally spent the last twenty-three days, six hours, and …" glancing at my watch, I add, "thirty-eight minutes wishing I could go back in time and do everything differently. If I could, I would not have been a coward, or an arse, or a liar. When you skidded into my arms, I would have said what was on my mind, which was that you are the most breathtaking woman I'd ever seen and that even though it was absolutely insane, I was pretty sure I never wanted to let you go. Then, of course, I would have gotten you a towel, like a proper gentleman, let you get dressed, and waited to see if you could possibly like me back. But my regrets are not your concern and I know that."

She nods. "Exactly."

"You should move on and find someone who's … not me."

"I will," she says, slathering butter on her bun and taking a bite.

"Good. You do that," I say, watching her sadly. "And I'll be hoping from afar that all your dreams come true."

Chapter Thirty-Nine

Aimée

I want to jump over the table and crawl into Noel's arms and beg him to never let me go. How can I feel like that after what he did? Have I no self-respect at all? To help resist my impulse, I eat three rolls in a row which gives my hands something else to do. It might also help fill me up. I don't think that bowl of soup is going to do the trick.

The sommelier brings two glasses of pink champagne to the table. "The 1996 Plenitude Dom Pérignon Rosé," he announces like it's the liquid equivalent of the Hope Diamond. As far as I know, it is.

Noel smiles up at him. "One of my favorites, thank you." He takes a slow sip while keeping his eyes trained on me. Then he picks up both glasses. With one, he toasts, "To love, may I never mess it up as royally again!" He clinks both glasses together and takes another sip.

I roll my eyes while reaching across the table to take one of the glasses. "I feel like I owe it to the universe to drink to that." I add, "I don't want some other poor woman to have to go through what I did." I feel an actual stabbing pain in my chest at the thought of him with another woman. Or is that from inhaling all those buns?

When the appetizers arrive, Noel asks our waiter for more rolls. I ate four. Then he pushes one of the plates in front of me while moving the soup into the middle of the table. I let him because, as God is my witness, I have never wanted to eat crab cakes so badly in my entire life. They look amazing.

"Only one," Noel cautions me. "I'll save you half of my sweetbreads." I'm not sure I'm that big on thymus gland, so I might just eat my soup at that point.

I cut a small bite of my crab cake and bring it to my nose. I can smell the heady bay seasoning and the citrusy-fresh mango chutney. Then I close my eyes and bring my fork to my mouth. Once the brine of the seafood and sweet fruit burst onto my tongue, I release a groan of pure unadulterated pleasure. I open my eyes to see Noel staring at me like I'm in the throes of some other pleasure entirely. "What? It's good," I tell him.

"Aimée Tompkins, my lovely caterer, do you remember why I didn't stand up and shake your hand properly that first day we met?" For clarification purposes, I suppose, he adds, "*After* you got dressed?"

I lower my gaze. He said he didn't want to embarrass himself because he was … that is to say … visibly interested. I peek at him again very slowly and nod my head.

"I'm suffering the same plight again. If you plan to keep moaning through this meal, I'm going to have to walk away and run my head under cold water in the loo." I'm valiantly trying not to smile when he adds, "The other diners could play ring toss as I dash by."

I burst out laughing despite my anger and hurry to shove another bite of crab cake into my mouth to stifle my mirth. We eat silently for a few minutes before I ask, "So how is it working with Walter Junior?"

"About as much fun as passing a kidney stone, I expect. The man has decided that we're destined to be best buddies and he wants to start hanging out after work hours."

"Ew. How are you going to get out of it?" I ask.

"If he doesn't buy my excuses of being too busy working on his building, I'm going to tell him my girlfriend hates his guts, and she won't let me go out with him." He smirks when asking, "You don't mind if he thinks we're still together, do you?"

I shake my head while taking a truly huge bite of crab cake. I've already eaten mine, so I dig into Noel's. "Whatever will help." I eventually tell him when I come up for air.

"It would help if you really were my girlfriend..." He lets the thought linger.

I pick up my glass of champagne and drink the whole thing in one gulp.

Our ever-vigilant sommelier comes over with a bottle and refills our glasses. Noel says, "What more can I do?" He sounds pained. "My apologies are sincere; my heart is broken; I am a shell of the man I once was." Then he pulls out all the stops. "Aimée, I still love you. So very much."

Tears spring to my eyes and I do my best to stop them. I cannot sit here and cry in front of him after he lied to me and made such a fool of me. "Pardon me," I manage to say before jumping up and fleeing out of the room.

I'm at the bathroom door before I realize Teisha is hot on my heels. "Girl, what now? It looked like you were having the time of your life until you bolted out of there like a lobster was nipping at your butt."

"Oh, T." I throw myself into her arms and sob. "He told me he still loves me!"

"Well? Do you still love him?"

"So much, but I can't reconcile how to forgive him. If our life together is based on a lie, how can I ever trust what comes next?"

"For the love of God, woman, you're dramatic. This isn't *Gone with the Wind* here; this is you and Noel in New York City making a mess that doesn't need making. If you get back together, I promise the worst thing that will happen is that I'll miss you because you'll never be at home. And while I might have once thought that to be a horrible thing, I now think I might like to invite Kwan over without you being there boohooing all over the throw pillows."

"How are things going with you guys?" I ask. "You've been pretty tight-lipped since the other night."

"What's to say? My nail man and I are eating a meal or two together and are having a nice time."

"Your nail man?" I look at her with one eyebrow raised in disbelief that she's trying to sell me that line.

"I'm pulling a *you*, when you and Noel got together. I'm keeping things close to the vest for now. But don't worry, if we confess our love to each other, I'll let you know." She wipes a tear from my eye before pinching my cheeks and asking, "Now, what are you going to do about him?"

"I don't know. I guess I'm going to finish dinner and see what happens. I just don't think I can forgive him."

We walk back into the dining room together, and I stop dead in my tracks when I see what Noel is up to.

Chapter Forty

Noel

I stand in the center of the dining room, holding a half-full flute, my heart pounding in my ears as I watch the servers fill the last of the champagne glasses I ordered for … well, everyone in the restaurant. It's my last chance and, by God, I'm going to make it count.

I glance over to the hall leading to the ladies' room and see it's go-time. Aimée and Teisha are huddled together, wearing matching expressions of confusion.

Well, this is it, you wanker. You better make this work.

Clearing my throat, I raise my voice so no one will miss a word of the humiliating display I'm about to give them. "Good evening, everyone. I apologize for interrupting your meal. My name is Noel Fitzwilliam and I am a very boring, straight-edged, workaholic Brit. I'm also very private. I don't even strike up a conversation with the person next to me on a flight, let alone an entire restaurant full of people. I detest being the center the of attention."

Okay, now's not the time to ramble. Just get to the point. "But recently, I met a woman who has changed my life. The sun is warmer when she's around; colors are more vivid; even food tastes better—especially gingersnaps." I gesture to her. "There she is. In the navy dress." I wait while everyone turns to look. "The only woman I have ever loved."

Good God, I'm sweating like a fat man in a sauna. "Unfortunately, I messed the entire thing up by lying to her. I was desperate to spend time with her and I was a total coward by pretending I was someone else."

"Boo!" a lady in a red dress yells.

I turn to my critic, "You are exactly right, madam. It was stupid and unforgivable."

A man at her table puts one hand next to his mouth and says, "Who'd you pretend to be? A prince or something so she'd think you have money?"

It is so hot in here. Like stiflingly hot. Why didn't I notice how bloody hot it was before? "Oh, um, I wasn't expecting questions actually, ummm … but no. I pretended to be my assistant."

"So you pretended you *didn't* have money?" the man asks, screwing up his face in confusion.

"Yes, but that's beside the point because—"

"Wait, wait, wait," the woman in red says. "For the sake of setting the proper scene, you're saying you do have money."

"I … I do all right, I suppose." Oh bollocks, this was the worst idea I've ever had. You know, other than the whole texting thing.

"Hey, he makes enough to buy each of us a glass of the good stuff," a man in the back corner yells, earning him a laugh.

I nod in his direction, uncomfortably. Then I continue, "The thing is, you should never lie, especially not to the woman you'd lay down your life for. But I did and she rightly showed me the door." Before people can start cheering her sensible decision, I quickly add, "My greatest regret is that I broke her trust. And so, Aimée, my love, I will respect your wishes, but if you will indulge me, I'd like to send you on your way with a little song by the great Ms. Whitney Houston."

I glance at Byron who's shaking his head and doing the "cut" sign across his neck repeatedly. Byron was there when I was asked to mouth the words to "Good King Wenceslas," and he hugged me after school when I had a bit of a cry about it. But that was a long time ago. Maybe the honesty of my feelings will magically make me better. Sod it, here I go …

"Iffffffff I … should stay, I would only be in your way …" I start to talk/sing slowly. Aimée looks like she's in physical pain. Maybe I should stop. No, no, no stopping. I need a grand gesture here—John-Cusack-with-a-boombox-blasting-Peter-Gabriel grand. Alas, I have no boombox, so I gird my loins and plug on.

"So I'll go but I know, I'll think of you …" and now I just say this bit because there's no way I can hit the right notes. "… every step of the way."

Christ, the talking is somehow worse. I never should have done this. And now for the chorus. I really have to go for it. I take a deep inhale then belt out, "AaaaannnnnddddddIIIIIIIIeeeeeeIIIIIIIeeeeeeeee eIIIIIIIIIIIIIII will always love you-hooooooooooooooo ooo ooo!"

Christ almighty, I'm bad. Peter starts toward me and joins in with his arms out to the sides as he belts out the chorus Pavarotti-style. I'm momentarily rendered mute, but then just knowing that his glorious baritone is going to drown me out, I let my volume increase.

Registering the shock on my face, Peter leans in and tells me, "I'm only a sommelier at night. I teach opera lessons during the day."

"Oh, very nice," I compliment, before we both turn back to Aimée and belt out the line about life treating her kind. By the time we get to the chorus again, most of the patrons have joined in, totally drowning me out, including Byron who is now behind me, pushing me toward the woman I love.

When I reach her, my heart leaps because I can see love shining in her eyes. After the last line is sung, everyone goes quiet as I'm sure they're rapt to see what the idiot Englishman is going to do now. I say, "My darling, I love you. I will always love you. But I understand if you can't give me another chance. I don't deserve it."

She blinks quickly. The tension in the air is so thick, I'm pretty sure even the kitchen staff are waiting with bated breath.

Aimée shakes her head. "I'm sorry. I just can't…"

She hurries past me, leaving me with a hundred or so people as witness to the exact moment my heart breaks forever. I turn and watch as she winds her way through the tables, then I speak up, "As you wish."

She stops where she is and puts her head down, then turns to me. "Really? You're going full *Princess Bride* on me?"

"I would go *Full Monty* on you if I thought it would help." Gauging her reaction to see if my stripping naked in front of a room full of strangers would be sufficient humiliation for her to forgive me—some of them have been filming me with their cameras for the YouTube video that will undoubtedly go viral by morning—I begin to unbutton my shirt.

"No." She lifts her hands in the air and lets them drop by her sides in frustration. "Dammit, Noel, you are the most infuriating man on the planet! Can't you see I'm trying to hate you?"

Byron and Teisha both shove me. I stumble a little then walk toward her, meeting her in the middle of the restaurant. When I reach her, she has tears running down her cheeks and I'm more than a little terrified she's going to go into the ugly cry … with the snot and everything, but she doesn't. She sighs and shakes her head at me. "I want to hate you, so *so* badly, but then you do something insane like totally humiliating yourself by singing Whitney Houston in front of all these people and … and … it was the most stupidly perfect thing you could do. I just … I just … I can't be mad at you anymore."

"Does that mean you'll come back to me?" I ask. Her answer holds the key to my happiness.

She shakes her head sadly.

It's like an atomic bomb has landed on my heart. When I can finally breathe again, a sob chokes me as I tell her, "I will never stop wanting you to have everything you desire in life, everything you deserve." I reach up and tentatively touch her cheek with the backs of my fingers, feeling her soft skin against mine. "I hope you find someone worthy of your love."

Aimée nods and sniffles. "Thanks, me too."

When she turns and walks out, I know, that just like Jerry McGuire I'll never be complete again. Byron comes to stand next to me and puts his arm on my shoulder. "That isn't how I thought this would play out."

"Me neither," I say, sucking in a breath.

"You should never have sung to her," he adds, with a little shake of his head. "Not Miss Whitney, anyway. That was a stretch."

I nod my head heavily as I pull my wallet out of my jacket pocket and hand it to him. "Can you pay my tab for me? I'm going to head out."

"Sure thing, Noel."

My shoulders slump as I keep my gaze on the carpet to avoid all the faces staring at me with abject pity. When I get outside onto the sidewalk, the cool evening air reminds me to breathe again. I turn right and start walking, not caring where I end up. When I'm about halfway down the block, I hear her call my name. I turn and see Aimée, smiling through her tears.

As she runs up to me, my entire body feels numb. Holding out one hand, she says, "Hi, I'm Aimée. I'm a caterer. I plan to be a huge success in my field, so I'm going to be very busy. Some might even say a workaholic." She continues, "I plan to get married someday, and have a bunch of kids, so if either of those ideas scare you—especially the first one—just say so because it's a deal-breaker."

I shake my head and grin, my entire chest feeling like it's going to explode with happiness.

She keeps talking. "I like long romantic walks to the fridge, puppies, and having my feet rubbed. I won't put up with being lied to because I'd never do that to someone I love."

I can't seem to find the right words. Is she coming back to me here? Now? Before I can ask, she continues, "I'm pretty sure you look like someone I could love."

"Aimée … I …"

"You said you wished more than anything that you could start over so I'm going to let you, but *just once*, you got that?"

Nodding my head, I wrap my arms around her. "Got it." I hold on tight, afraid to believe in my good fortune. But when she doesn't dissolve like an ethereal mist, I finally believe this is really happening. "I'm Noel and I think you're the most beautiful woman I've ever laid eyes on. I like watching you dance around the kitchen while you cook and making you laugh. I love rubbing your feet and your legs, and your … back. I adore hearing you moan when you eat, so much so, that I want to take you to every good restaurant in the entire world, just to hear that sound." I take a deep breath before saying, "I will never lie to you, not even in those situations where you may actually want me to, like say … you buy some trousers that aren't exactly flattering, and you just want me to say they look great on you. I'll tell you the God's honest truth."

Aimée tilts her head, her eyes narrowing a little. "Whoa, let's not get carried away. White lies used to preserve my self-esteem are perfectly acceptable."

Grinning, I move in closer and gently brush my lips against hers. "I don't know … I'd hate to risk it."

Laughing, she says, "Shut up and kiss me already."

And I do.

And she kisses me right back. Before we forget we're standing on a public street in the heart of New York City, I pull back and say, "I will always love you."

"Unfortunately, I'm always going to love you too. But no more singing in public, okay? Like never, ever."

"You poor, poor woman," I murmur against her lips. "Do you want to go back to my place? I have mint chocolate chip ice cream."

"Yeah, I do," she says, grinning.

"Wait, I need to do one thing first," I say. Dragging her back down the block, I pull her into the restaurant, and straight to the dining room. Raising my voice, I yell, "She changed her mind! She loves me after all!"

The patrons all stare, but they don't stand and start clapping like I thought they would. A couple of them give me the thumbs up, but then they all go back to eating. The lady in the red dress, who is now on her way out, pats me on the arm. "That's nice, dear."

"Thank you," I say, my face flaming with embarrassment. "I'm quite thrilled actually," I say to her back as she walks away.

"Okay, she's gone," Aimée says. "You done?"

"Yeah, I just thought they'd all want to know for some reason," I tell her.

She tugs my hand in the direction of the door. "It's New York, honey. Nobody cares."

Epilogue

"Noel, would you hurry up already?" I ask my boyfriend who's dawdling like I've never seen before.

"I cannot believe we're going to be on the *Today Show*. It's rather mortifying, no?" he grumbles.

"You're the one who executed the whole restaurant scene, not me." Grabbing my purse off the console, I add, "Forty million views in ten months is pretty impressive."

He cringes. "What would happen if we didn't go?"

"Oh, we're going!" I tell him. "Think of the exposure for Nibbles and Noshes! I'm going to drop the name of my company at least three times while we're on the air."

"You're already busier than I can stand," he says while walking toward me to pull me into his arms. "If you take on any more business, I'll never see you."

"Says the man designing the most innovative skyscraper in the history of skyscrapers."

"I barely work, compared to you!"

"Don't worry. Teisha is hiring new people in preparation for the spike in business we're about to have. Now, come on, we're supposed to be at

Rockefeller Center by five and it's already four thirty."

Noel grabs his jacket. "Fine, but after this, no more. I don't want them having us back for a yearly reunion or anything."

It only takes ten minutes for the town car to reach 1 Rockefeller Plaza this time in the morning. Tanya, the producer in charge of our segment, meets us in the lobby. "Thank goodness you're here!" she says while tapping on her watch.

"Are we late?" I ask nervously.

"Not yet, but we need to get you into makeup and brief you on how your segment is going to go. Follow me," she says while walking away from us like she's competing for the title of Speed Walking Champion of the World.

Tanya shows us to our dressing room, which is a small room with a loveseat and a television. "Makeup will come and get you in a few minutes. After that, wait here until I come back. Just be casual and relaxed and be prepared for Hoda to ask you a thousand questions. I swear, a million of your YouTube hits were hers alone."

Well, that certainly sets us up to be relaxed. *What was she thinking?*

After Tanya leaves, Noel says, "We could still make a run for it."

"I'm considering it," I tell him. Unfortunately, we don't have a chance to seriously discuss that option before the hair and makeup people come in. They lead us to a long counter with mirrors covering the wall above it, and several chairs like you find in the beauty parlor.

I'm so nervous, I'm practically shaking. The lady doing my makeup says, "Just sit still and be calm. Everyone is nervous before going on."

"Do you have any idea who the other guests are today?" I ask, hoping to think about something else, anything other than my impending introduction to Hoda and her bazillion viewers.

"Yeah, we've got that old lady from Sagaponack who crocheted the world's biggest potholder, and Dolly Parton."

"Dolly Parton? As in *the* Dolly Parton?" I ask on the off chance she's talking about someone's golden retriever named Dolly Parton. Alas, I'm not holding my breath as this is the *Today Show*.

"Yup, *the* Dolly Parton," she says while liberally dotting my face with concealer. "She's always a lot of fun."

"Do you get to do her makeup, too?" I ask in awe.

"Dolly brings her own crew," she answers, as I wonder about the amount of makeup that woman must go through in a year. She always looks perfect.

By the time Noel and I are both back in our little dressing room, I'm on the verge of hyperventilating. "Why are we doing this again?" I ask him.

"You've decided you won't rest until you're the official caterer to the entire borough of Manhattan. Or so you've said," he reminds me.

"Right. Yes." I sit down on the loveseat and put my head between my knees to keep from passing out. We only have minutes before Tanya is back.

"Okay, let's go get you mic'd up. You're on in five."

"Five minutes?" I gasp. Holy crap, the room starts to spin. Apparently, Tanya doesn't have time for my drama because she turns and walks away.

Noel drags me after her. Behind the set, a burly guy named Tony runs a black cord up the back of my shirt and clips it to the collar. "Watch your hands there, fella," Noel tells him. Tony ignores him. He probably gets to second base with thousands of women a year doing this.

Like I'm underwater, I hear a very muffled Hoda say, "My next guests nearly broke the Internet with their very public and very romantic make up scene at a restaurant right here in New York. They've had over forty-million hits on their video ..." She pauses for affect. "And I'm guessing by the end of today, they'll probably have another forty."

Dear. Sweet. Jesus. Comeformenow and don't drag your feet.

Hoda stands up. "Normally I'd have my guests sit here with me, but I thought for kicks we'd set up a restaurant table for them. Aimée and Noel," she calls off stage. "Will you join me?"

We walk out onto the set to find a small bistro table with two chairs. There are candles burning and there's a breadbasket on the table. What in the heck is going on here? Hoda gestures for us to sit down before turning to a makeshift stage that's set up nearby. She says, "Noel, I think I'll let you take it from here."

WHAT?!

Noel stands up and walks to the stage but not before blowing me a kiss. When he gets there, he taps the microphone and says, "Aimée, I promised no more big scenes." *He did, too.* "But I believe you left me a little leeway in that promise."

"I told you that you could lie to me if I looked fat in my pants," I remind him. "Please don't tell me we're on national television for that?" I sound equal amounts annoyed and terrified.

Noel answers. "I'd like to introduce you to the woman who wrote the song that brought us back together." Pregnant pause. "Ms. Dolly Parton."

Dolly walks out onto the stage in all her glory. Her smile stretches from ear-to-ear. She waves to me and says, "I am so pleased to be a part of this day, honey." Then out of nowhere, she starts to sing "I Will Always Love You." I sit in rapt awe that this is really happening. When she gets to the refrain, she nudges Noel in the ribs to join in.

Make. It. Stop.

Dolly must feel similarly because after six or so notes, she reaches over and turns Noel's microphone off. By the time the song is over, I'm bawling, cringing, and otherwise too stunned to speak.

Hoda approaches the stage and shakes Dolly's hand before turning to Noel. "Carry on, Noel."

My one true love approaches me and drops to his knee before me and the free world, who is currently watching us on television. He says, "Aimée, my love, as I've mentioned time and time again, I *will* always love you. Not only are you the best caterer in all the land,"—he turns to the camera and says,

"Nibbles and Noshes in Manhattan,"—before turning back to me and pulling a Tiffany blue ring box out of his jacket and continuing, "you are the love of my life and I don't want to wait another minute before asking you to be my wife."

I sit there in complete shock. Seriously, my mouth is wide open. You could toss peanuts into it and I wouldn't notice. "Aimée, will you marry me?" he asks.

All the synapses in my brain start to fire at once. There appears to be an alarming short-circuit afoot. Dolly Parton encourages from the sidelines, "Go on, hon. Tell the man you can't live without him either."

As Noel puts the most beautiful diamond I have ever seen on my finger, I answer, "I do. I mean, I will. I mean, YES!!!"

Noel picks me up and twirls me around before saying, "You won't be sorry."

"What happened to no more big scenes?" I ask again.

"This is the last one, I promise." The slow wink he gives me makes me nervous, but at the moment I don't care. I am going to marry the most wonderful man in the entire world and by golly we are going to live happily-ever-after if it kills us.

THE END

AFTERWORD

A Note from Melanie and Whitney

Thank you so much for taking the time to read Noel and Aimee's story! If you enjoyed it, please take a moment to leave a review. Reviews are a true gift to writers. They are the best way for other readers to find our work.

If you aren't already signed up for our newsletters, please do so! This way we can keep you apprised of new releases, promotions, etc.

Whitney Dineen – www.whitneydineen.com/newsletter

Melanie Summers – www.melaniesummersbooks.com

Need more laughs? Try:

The Text God:
An Accidentally in Love
Story, Book 2

Text and you shall receive...

Jen Flanders moved to New York to be an artist. This translates into walking dogs for money, practicing yoga for sanity, and hitting up her friends at a local bakery to supplement her diet. Rent is due and she's running out of cash. After begging the universe for a sign that help is on the way, her phone pings with an incoming text. GOD: You can do it; I believe in you!

Attorney Gabriel Oliver Daly agreed to mentor a friend's younger sister. Unbeknownst to him, after losing her phone, said sister uses her dog walker's phone to text him about a job offer. He responds enthusiastically.

Jen can't believe GOD is actually texting her! But who is she to question the ways of the universe? On the first day of texting, GOD gets her a job that will keep her afloat. On the second and third days he offers even more help.

Gabriel starts to think his friend's sister might be too flighty to make it in the legal jungle of New York. Why exactly does she need a survival job?

Wasn't she supposed to be interviewing for a position as a junior lawyer? And why is she texting him random (not to mention *very personal*) stuff all the time?

When they finally meet, Jen realizes GOD isn't a deity but a divinely handsome lawyer. A complete stranger has answered all her prayers. After all, God does move in mysterious ways.

About the Authors

WHITNEY DINEEN

Whitney Dineen is a rock star in her own head. While delusional about her singing abilities, there's been a plethora of validation that she's a fairly decent author (AMAZING!!!). After winning many writing awards and selling nearly a kabillion books (math may not be her forte, either), she's decided to let the voices in her head say whatever they want (sorry, Mom). She also won a fourth-place ribbon in a fifth-grade swim meet in backstroke. So, there's that.

Whitney loves to play with her kids (a.k.a. dazzle them with her amazing flossing abilities), bake stuff, eat stuff, and write books for people who "get" her. She thinks french fries are the perfect food and Mrs. Roper is her spirit animal.

MELANIE SUMMERS

Melanie Summers lives in Edmonton, Canada, with her husband, three kiddos, and two cuddly dogs. When she's not writing, she loves reading (obviously), snuggling up on the couch with her family for movie night (which would not be complete without lots of popcorn and milkshakes), and long walks in the woods near her house. Melanie also loves shutting down restaurants with her girlfriends. Well, not literally shutting them down, like calling the health inspector or something. More like just staying until they turn the lights off.

Made in the USA
Las Vegas, NV
03 April 2021